Every
I Love You
ISN'T TRUE

RaSheeda Bryant- McNeil

authorHOUSE®

AuthorHouse™
1663 Liberty Drive
Bloomington, IN 47403
www.authorhouse.com
Phone: 1 (800) 839-8640

Published by AuthorHouse   09/14/2015

ISBN: 978-1-5049-5049-7 (sc)
ISBN: 978-1-5049-2183-1 (e)

Library of Congress Control Number: 2015915103

Print information available on the last page.

Any people depicted in stock imagery provided by Thinkstock are models, and such images are being used for illustrative purposes only. Certain stock imagery © Thinkstock.

This book is printed on acid-free paper.

Dedication

To the man who worked all his life doing what
he had to do
so that I could live my life doing what I want to
do, which is write.
I love you Daddy!
Rest in Heaven
Thomas Jefferson Bryant Sr.

Acknowledgments

Authors Carl Weber, Tracey Brown, Mary B. Morrison,

&

Ashley & JaQuavis

Thank you for having enough courage to share your style of writing which empowered me to share mine.

PROLOGUE

"Uhm, baby, yes, take all this dick in your mouth."

"I'm sorry, Daddy, for being a naughty girl," I said seductively while preparing to give my man the best lollipop job of his life. I loved it when he talked dirty to me while I was pleasing him. It seemed he'd finally figured out that I was the one for him. After weeks of us arguing and him denying me of this good dick, I was going to suck and swallow every ounce of cum out of him. I wanted to feel him inside of me so bad, but the occasion wouldn't allow it. I was already dripping down my leg from the excitement of tasting him. If I let him put it in, I knew for a fact that cum and wetness would be all over my dress and my Beyoncé ass. I wouldn't have time to clean up before the wedding music started, but it didn't matter, because that night, he would be all mine. I couldn't wait.

Suddenly, I heard footsteps stop right outside the closed door, breaking my concentration. He must have sensed I was about to stop performing, and to my surprise, he grabbed me harder by the head and started groaning. A part of me wanted to stop. I was scared someone would walk in; however, my pussy started thumping with excitement as I realized he was turned on more by the idea that someone was at the door. "I'm about to cum. I'm about to cum! I'm about to cum!!!" he said, his voice growing louder each time he said it. Going faster and deeper, he filled my mouth with warm cum. I smiled on the inside and swallowed. Then I seductively started licking his head to make sure I got all of the cum. I heard the door open just as I was cum'n, but since it didn't seem to faze him, I hadn't even stopped to look. As he was filling my mouth with what could have been our kids, I looked up at him and into his eyes. His eyes were mesmerizing. As he looked in the direction of the dark oak door the church had just replaced, he had a satisfied look in his eyes and a smile on his face.

The next thing I knew, I felt something cold and hard on the side of my head. "Cocked and loaded," I heard a firm voice say. "You might as well stay down, bitch, because you're not getting back up."

CHAPTER 1

Adrianna

I knew I was supposed to be crying my eyes out, playing the devastated fiancée role; however, I couldn't help but wonder why this bitch Diamond was crying more than everyone else at this damn funeral. As I sat there pretending to be listening to the pastor, my mind replayed how it all began.

Diamond ran the naked safe house for my fiancé, Bossman, and my sister Jullian's fiancé, West. I had never liked the bitch but put up with her late-night and all-day phone calls to my man, because as long as she was helping to make our money, I was able to spend it. Bossman and

West had her check in every hour to confirm via phone call or text that everything was on track. West had the day shift for all confirmations, from sunup to sundown, and Bossman handled all confirmations from sundown to sunup.

One late night, I was about to go in on her ass for calling when Bossman let me in on a well-kept secret: Diamond was West's jump-off. My first reaction was to call my sister immediately and tell her about her man, but Bossman encouraged me otherwise. "Wifey," he said, taking the phone out of my hand and looking me straight in my green eyes, "in this game of life, there are sacrifices to be made, and this is one of them."

With a fuck-out-of-here face, I rhetorically said, "What does that have to do with my loyalty to my sister, Boss? Do you actually think I'm gonna sit on this vital information? I can't have my sister out here thinking she's the only when, in fact, she is just the top-notch bitch," I said with my head cocked to the side and my right hand on my hip.

Truth be told, my sister Jullian was a ten, but I'd heard Diamond was a ten in the sheets and a ten on the streets. That hoe had one up, which meant competition, and competition had to be eliminated.

He knew I was about to be on ten. He was leaning against the wall, hands in his pockets, wearing an all-white linen outfit that looked as if it had been tailor-made to his chocolate skin. He took his hands out of his pockets; licked his smooth, thick lips; rubbed his chin; and then proceeded to walk over to me like a boss. I loved the way this man walked. Hell, I loved everything about him.

"Look, Adrianna, Jullian has a happy home. West makes sure she has everything emotionally and especially financially. What nigga in the game make sure he come home every night before two in the morning just out of respect for his girl?" He spoke with the utmost respect for West. I cocked my head to the side and said, "A real one." I rolled my eyes and began to turn over in bed, when I felt Boss grab the shit out of me.

"Adrianna, don't make me call you out of your name, and don't make me lay hands on you. I have never hit a woman unless she was a fiend, but you about one second from feeling me. You hear me?" His piercing eyes told me he wasn't playing, so I shut the fuck up and closed my eyes, hoping he would just get off of me.

I couldn't take one more sniff of his alcoholic breath, but the smell of alcohol was a signal for Ms. Kitty to start thumping. She knew that when he came home tipsy or drunk, she was going to get licked until she came all over his mouth. I quickly acted submissive, because the sooner I acted as if I agreed, the sooner I could put my plan into action.

As soon as Bossman went to sleep, my ass was dialing Jullian's phone. Instead of going to sleep or trying to get some, he grabbed his phone to call Diamond back. I heard him explaining why his voice sounded so excited, as if he owed her an explanation or something. "I'm cool, baby girl. I just had to take care of the home team first before I could answer." He looked back at me with a devilish grin, grabbed his nine, and then left the room for some privacy.

I knew he was heading to the media room for privacy. I never went in there. I didn't have time to watch TV. I was about my money. The only thing I wanted to watch was my money stack. He had the room decked out with mirrors all over, so when he was watching a movie, it showed in the mirrors as well. It was a man's room, with a long black-leather sectional, every game device one could imagine, and a fully stocked minibar. I hadn't been in there since we moved in. That was his room, and I had mine. We had an office on the first floor beside the library, but he never used it. The library was my room. I monitored my shoe-and-accessory store, DivaStar, from my office, even though I went in every day. I'd learned from Bossman that in order for people to respect you as the boss, you had to be on the scene like the boss. That was one thing he taught me.

To my surprise, he didn't go to the media room; instead, I heard him at the bar, pouring himself a drink. Thank God our master bedroom was on the bottom floor because I could sneak up on his ass and bust him in the head if necessary. As I tiptoed down the hallway toward the kitchen, I stubbed my darn pinkie toe. At times like this, I hated that I was light skinned, because I bruised easily.

He was so engulfed in his conversation that he didn't even hear me say, "Oh shit!"

Like a spy, I hid behind the second staircase, which was located between the breakfast area and the kitchen. After a pause, I heard him say, "Nah, it ain't like that. I'm the man of this castle just like I'm the king of the safe house. For the last time, Diamond, don't have your punk-ass brother, Sly, up at my spot. I don't trust those up-and-coming niggas. They don't respect the golden rules of the streets."

While he listened to Diamond's reply, I saw him take a sip of Henny and then, clutching his jaw, slam the glass down on the bar's black-marble countertop. He took a long breath and started rubbing his hands and popping his knuckles. That meant he was getting all amped up. Then he started rubbing his chin as if he were thinking about what he was about to say to shut her down completely. "We take corner boys like him out for even sniffing around our spot. He suspect. I know that's your fam, but I'm not trying to go to jail to become a thumb-in-the-booty-hole nigga. You feel me? Baby girl, I'm not gonna repeat myself, and that's final."

Click.

I thought, *Did this nigga just call her "baby girl"? I know I didn't just hear him call her my nickname.* I came around the staircase and was in his face so fast that I didn't even remember walking toward him. "Baby girl? Baby girl—that's what you call every female now, Boss?"

I prepared myself for him to start a full-blown fight, but he did just the opposite. When I got close enough, he picked me up from under my ass and threw me onto the bar. He untied my white silk robe to show my hard nipples through my matching white silk gown underneath. I saw his nature rise, and immediately, Ms. Kitty started thumping again.

His chocolate skin was smooth rubbing up against mine. He lifted my gown, leaned me back, and tasted me until I came all over him. In one sweeping motion, he flipped me over, wrapped my jet-black ponytail around his hand for a firm grip, and gave it to me from the back until we both were completely satisfied.

Damn, I love my nigga.

However, I would never love a man more than I loved myself. I believed that no matter how much a man said he loved you, he would never love you more than he loved himself. All the hoes he had on the side only confirmed my belief. It was cool though, because if he ever left me,

I already had my eye on plan B. Plan B was a motherfucker too.

Bossman and West were two of the few kingpins who never had any of their spots hit. Charlotte, North Carolina, was known to breed stick-up boys, so even though they'd never gotten hit up, they knew that one day someone would try it.

Well, that day came—in broad daylight—and of course, there were no witnesses.

Now there I was, looking at my future husband in an all-white Alexander Amosu suit, his favorite brown-and-gold Prada shades, and tan-and-brown size-16 Prada dress shoes. I scanned him up and down and couldn't help but smile inside at his Bossman stature and the look on his face. *A Rick Ross lookalike would be an understatement,* I thought while staring at him as he lay in his all-white diamond-studded casket.

We just buried West yesterday, and Jullian was crushed. His family took care of everything, including her. West had made sure they knew how important Jullian was when he was alive, just in case he ever had to leave this earth early.

Jullian looked just like Nia Long from a distance, with her stance and sassy, short cut. She had the prettiest clear brown skin, like that of her birth mother, Beverly, and our mother, Josephine. Jullian had a different mother but had been raised with Charisma and I. She had our Banks family signature: slanted eyes. Everyone in the family had black eyes except for my father, Warren, and I. I'd always wanted my mother's and sisters' complexions. My sister Charisma was light brown, and Jullian was caramel brown. I was the only light-skinned one with freckles out of the bunch. Truly, I was like my father's twin. I knew I was sexy. There was nothing wrong with being light skinned, but I just wanted to fit in with my sisters. When we took pictures, I was always the bright one in the bunch. Unless people met my father, when I was with my mom and sisters in public, they would stare at me as if wondering if I were adopted or something. Charisma was the favorite in the family. She tried her best to be humble about her achievements, but she was too good to be fucking true. She had won best-looking female, most likely to succeed, best dressed, and homecoming queen every year. I had been in her shadow all through high school, since we were in the same grade. She was one year older than I was, but I skipped fourth grade.

Charisma wasn't the only smart one in the family. I'd always won most popular because of my "I don't give a fuck, because I'm going to do what I want to do, so let's have fun" attitude. Jullian was two years behind us and had her own crowd of fans. She'd won best dressed and most-popular female almost every year at school. Jullian was the youngest, and she was exactly who she showed you she was. I always felt competition, especially from Charisma. She never said she was better, but I knew she thought it. She made me feel as if I had gotten molested because I was the weaker one. "Why couldn't he just think I was the prettiest one, Charisma? You can't stand the fact that someone chose me!" I shouted at her the day the family found out. I confided in her first on our front steps, because she was my big sister, and all she could say was "I wonder why you and not me." No one wanted to be molested, but for some sick reason, I gloated about the fact that someone had finally chosen me over her.

She'd already snatched our neighbor Rashad Jones from me when he moved in. While looking at his family through the window as they were moving in, I said how fine he was. She rolled her eyes and said, "Looks like another pretty boy to me." As we were talking, we lost sight of where he went, and the doorbell rang. No one knew it, but I was sore from being touched by Mr. Donald, so I didn't race Charisma to the door, as I normally would have. I thought the visitor was probably just a Jehovah's Witness anyway, because I had seen some of them walking around the neighborhood that day. To my surprise, it was Rashad Jones. His parents had made him come over to ask what time the bus came in the morning. Charisma walked outside to talk to him, and they had been inseparable ever since.

After I told her the rest of the details about Mr. Donald, she just looked at me with a shocked face. As she got up off the porch swing, she kissed me on the forehead and said, "You know I have to tell Mama, right? You don't have to tell this story twice." Then she went into the house, leaving me to my thoughts.

Half of me thought, *Why does she have to be the freaking hero and go tell Mama?* The other half of me was glad I didn't have to repeat the story twice. That night, Mama sent Charisma off for nine months to go live with my aunt. I figured she wanted to protect her since she hadn't been able to protect me.

The abuse emotionally drained me. Little did they know, Mr. Donald had not only molested me but also raped me. I was still a virgin when his adult hands touched me. I kept going back because he kept saying, "If you let me feel it one more time, I won't ask again."

After the third time, my thirteen-year-old brain said, *He will never stop*, so I concocted a master plan. Mr. Donald was only twenty, but Mama had taught us to use the titles Mr. and Ms. for anyone who was considered grown. All of the teenage girls in the neighborhood thought he was fine, with his light-brown complexion and chiseled face. I came to find out he was doing all of the little fast teenage girls in the neighborhood too. He used to tell me I was different because I was a virgin, and he loved to look into my green eyes. He was always sweet and gentle to me. I told him no every time, but deep down, I wanted a man to love me. I felt conflicted. During our last encounter, I figured out that the more I said no, the more he got turned on. I wanted his attention but not that attention. After he came, I said, *pulling my panties up*, "Mr. Donald, my aunt Mary didn't come." I rubbed my belly, and in my little-girl voice, I whispered, "I think I'm pregnant."

I figured that would get him to stop for sure, and I was right. Just as my father ran off after he found out my mother was pregnant with me, Mr. Donald disappeared. He sat up from the bed so quickly that I thought he was going to come choke me. I immediately started thinking of an escape route out of his bedroom. However, he didn't even look at me when he spoke. He looked up—ironically, he looked to the ceiling, as if he were talking to God for a moment, asking him what he had gotten himself into. Throwing me my yellow sundress and matching training bra, still avoiding eye contact, he yelled, "Go home, and never come back! If you tell anybody—and I mean anybody—I will kill you!" I was surprised that he raised his voice. He never raised his voice at me. I was shocked, but deep down, I smiled because I would never have to sleep with him again. Firmly, he said while lighting a cigarette, "Remember to go out the back door. I don't want anyone seeing you leave."

Without another word, I hurried out of there. A 'For Sale' sign was in his yard the next day, and I never saw him again. Charisma didn't have to stay away after all. It had killed her to leave Rashad. She begged Mama to let her come home. After nine months, she did, but by that time, the Jones family had moved. In the midst of reminiscing, I felt someone pull my hair back off of my shoulders and place it behind my back. It was Charisma. "Hi, Sis. Do you want to come stay with me for a couple of days? I know you don't want to go home to an empty house. Darnelle and I are here for you if you need us," she said with sincerity.

Who the fuck is she to speak for Darnelle? I thought. *She is not his wife yet. Hoes kill me, claiming men as theirs without the last name.* I answered without looking away from the casket. "That is so thoughtful of you two." I decided to play her little fairy-tale game, so I included Darnelle in my response as well. I loved her, but I was going to show her ass one day that she wasn't the only queen in this family. "I promise I won't stay long," I said.

Flipping her hair, Charisma said, "Darnelle is in and out, so it's all good. You know he's not getting any until we get married anyway, so it's not like you will run across anything improper." She chuckled. Charisma was a virgin and always kept reminding me that she'd waited for her Prince Charming. They'd decided not to live together until they were married. I applauded the bitch, but damn, could I live? I didn't want to be reminded of her fairy-tale ending all the damn time. I couldn't believe fine-ass Darnelle had even waited. Just like Charisma, that nigga was too good to be true.

Mama, looking as if she could be related to Diahann Carroll, shushed us with her pointer finger and told us that the preacher was speaking. That meant "Shut up, or I will shut you up." Since we couldn't finish our conversation, I blew Charisma a kiss to let her know that I loved her for being my sister.

After the service, I remembered that Diamond hadn't cried a single tear at West's funeral. My mama leaned over and whispered, "Maybe the death of two of her closest people in the game is really getting to her." It was as if my mama could read my mind or something. My sister Jullian must have felt sorry for Diamond as well, because she held and rocked her almost the entire time during the church service. However, now that we were at the graveside, Jullian had an "I don't give a fuck about that bitch" look on her face when she looked at Diamond. Maybe she'd found out that Diamond was West's side chick and had been for years. Yeah, I had known about it, but why tell my sister? West had spoiled the shit out of her, come home every night, shown love to her and the entire family, never had a hoe call her, and planned on making her his wife. All he'd talked about was her. She never had to deal with jump-offs, late-night phone calls, other women sending Facebook messages, or baby mamas, as I had. Bossman had made sure he made it home before the sun came up—right before the sun came up. That nigga had thought he deserved a trophy for that shit too.

The funeral was over, and everyone was heading to his or her car to meet up at our home. Charisma and her fiancé, Darnelle, led the way. Everybody and their mama forgot they were at a funeral for a moment to admire her Lisa Raye swag and our signature Banks Beyoncé ass as she walked by through the grass. I might have gotten our father's green eyes, but she had gotten my mother's sexy, dark, slanted come-hither eyes. Charisma was only a few months away from graduating from the Charlotte School of Law—a lawyer who was about to marry a lawyer. She was going to be a beast too. She'd met Darnelle at the Mecklenburg County Courthouse, where she was a probation officer. She was in love. All of that happiness was taking to her hips too. She looked more voluptuous all of a sudden. Her breasts looked much fuller than normal. However, being in love with a woman never stopped a man from being a man, in my book. Every man had a weak moment at least once a day. If the right bitch caught him during that moment, he would fall. Men never learned to avoid a moment of pleasure in order to avoid the heartache of a lifetime. They always used their one pass to cheat, and if Charisma thought Darnelle wouldn't use his, she was more delusional than I thought. He was tall, wealthy, smart, dark, and handsome. He was a partner at his family's law firm: Mitchell, Reeves, and Associates. His father was a sitting judge in Mecklenburg County. Darnelle was every successful woman's dream, but my belief was "Fuck love, but love money. Men ain't shit!" Mr. Donald taught me that earlier on. At the end of the day, love would fuck you over. Men were a dime a dozen. I felt we should use them and pass them, just as they did to us. Although Charisma was a virgin, all she did was talk about his dick and head game during girls' night out. Apparently, he was nine inches, had a long tongue, and knew what to do with it. I felt that information was something she'd better keep in her back pocket before another woman came in like a thief in the night and stole him.

Bentleys, Mercedes, Range Rovers, Lexus', BMWs, and a numerous array of luxury cars were all lined up to exit the graveyard. None of them compared to the white custom-made Fisker Karma that Boss had. We all had on all white because that had always been Bossman's request for his funeral someday. When his parents were murdered due to his father being in the game, everyone had worn all black, and Boss had thought that was the most depressing thing. He'd told me to promise him that if he had to say, "Rest in peace," I would make sure he and everyone at his funeral wore all white. I put on Alicia Keys' "If I Ain't Got You" and followed the family limo. Boss had always told me you should drive your own vehicle just in case, no matter the circumstances. He'd taught me that I had to be in control at all times, no matter what. Since the Banks family, my family, was the only family he'd had outside of his estranged brothers, they rode in the limo, which was, of course, all white. "Dammit, I forgot to place my one white rose on his coffin," I said. I'd laid it on the grass beside my chair when we were throwing the red roses onto the coffin. I wanted it to be the last rose he was given. I was glad I'd driven my own car. "Boss, you taught me well, babe," I said with a smile as I whipped my all-white Bentley coupe around to head back to the graveside.

When I was pulling up, I noticed that Diamond's all-white Mercedes truck had not left. I thought, *Damn, I don't like the bitch, but she could have come to the family house to eat. Even dogs eat crumbs from the master's table.*

She didn't see me pull up and walk up from behind her, because she was on her knees beside Boss's grave, still holding on to her red rose. Crying and sniffling, she said, "I'm so sorry, Boss. My stupid-ass brother knew better than to kill you. When I found out that you were going to propose to Adrianna, I lost it!"

My blood pressure immediately shot through the roof. I couldn't even tell if I was breathing at that point. I said to myself, "*What this bitch just say?*" I took off my diamond earrings and, boiling inside, threw them down with my Jimmy Choo clutch purse.

"Remember our trips to Jamaica and to the Bahamas? We danced all night long and made love even longer," Diamond said. She stood up and started dancing like the Caribbean women they had seen on their trip, and I started removing my diamond-studded stilettos. "I just wanted to hit you where it hurt, and the only way I knew to do that was through your pockets!" she yelled through her sniffling and crying. Then she sadly said, "I never wanted Sly to kill you, Boss. I just lost it when you showed me that big-ass engagement ring for Adrianna. I felt like shit, because when you opened the box, I thought it was for me. I swear I didn't want him to kill you. Shit just went wrong, and I—"

I clocked that bitch in the back of her head with my heel. I hit that bitch so hard that she fell on top of the casket in the grave. As she was trying to crawl out of the grave, I yelled, "Bitch, you been laying with him—you might as well lay your ass down with him now!" She was desperately trying to crawl out of the grave. I sat there and watched her struggle with a sinister smile on my face. Her all-white Chanel dress was covered with dirt stains. When her hands reached the top of the grave, she reached out for me to help her. Instead, I picked up the first thing I saw—the graveside shovel—and hit her with all my might, knocking her back down onto the casket.

I walked away like a G and didn't utter a word to anybody. Real Gs moved in silence. If I hadn't left my gun in the car, I would have put a bullet in that bitch and thrown enough dirt on her body so that they would have buried her with his dumb ass. I loved Boss, but I would never have let myself fall in love with him. That is how your heart gets broken, and I didn't have the energy to repair a broken heart. I knew that no matter how much I could have loved him, he would never have been one hundred with me. Now that my boo was gone, plan B was in full effect. Soon I was going to show my ace in my back pocket, and when I made this play, I would be the last woman standing.

CHAPTER 2

Charisma

"Baby, give me a second," I said on the way to the funeral, leaning over the side of the car, bracing myself to vomit for the third time that day. Ever since my sisters and I had had to identify Bossman's and West's bodies, I had been throwing up. I'd been a probation officer for seven years, but I had never seen a fresh dead body. I saw them either alive or casket sharp. Boss and West had had at least twenty bullets in them apiece. Whoever had wanted them dead had really wanted them dead.

"Baby, take your time. Everyone hasn't even arrived yet," Darnelle said in his most comforting voice with his right hand on the small of my back.

Trying my best to just hurry up and throw up in order to get it over with, I placed my finger down my throat and gagged. It worked, and I'd have been damned if one drop had hit my Jimmy Choo Greta lamé stilettos Darnelle had just gotten me from DivaStar. Taking a mini bottle of Scope mouthwash out of my overnight bag, from Darnelle's house, I asked who had arrived. I wanted to see if I had enough time to fix my face, because I felt I looked flushed from all of the throwing up.

"Adrianna and Jullian are already sitting down," he said, seemingly trying to observe my face to see if I was feeling better after vomiting.

"And my mama?" I asked.

"Mrs. Josephine, Aunt Diane, and your baby cousin Dream are pulling up behind us now with Mr. Joseph," he said with urgency. He knew my mother would be overly concerned if she saw that

I was sick. I hurried up and got myself together and came from the side of the car to meet Mama and Joseph.

"Hi, sweetie. Are you okay?" my mama asked as soon as she opened her car door. That meant she had seen it all, and there was no way out of having this conversation.

"Yes, Mama. I think it was something I ate."

Darnelle cut his eye at me with a look of shock on his face. He knew I was lying, because I hadn't eaten anything for breakfast that morning. He'd gotten up early and served me breakfast in bed. The food had looked good, but I'd only been able to stomach one slice of toast and some orange juice.

Even with all of the commotion, I couldn't help but notice how beautiful Dream was. She looked just as I had as a teenager. She had beautiful skin, long hair, and Chinese eyes with long lashes. She looked innocent. Auntie Diane had raised her well. She was a straight-A student who was respectful and too involved in the church to have time for anything else. My aunt made sure of that. She was going to say the closing prayer that day at Bossman's funeral. She said she had known since she was seven that she was called to be a pastor.

I rubbed my fingers through Dream's freshly highlighted hair, beaming like a proud mother, thinking about how proud I was.

"You sure are filling out that white Chanel dress I got you for Christmas," Mama told me with a slight smile, lifting her head so that I could see the look on her face under her white lace church hat. My aunt cosigned. My mother reminded me of Diahann Carroll in the way she dressed and in her mannerisms; however, her voice was soothing like Felicia Rashad's. She used her calming voice now just as she did at the hospital, where she was an RN. I knew she was waiting for me to confirm to her that I'd let Darnelle get some milk and cookies since we were engaged, but before I could tell her no, Mr. Joseph interrupted our conversation.

"It looks like they are about to start, ladies. Let me have your hand, honey. I don't want you to fall walking in those heels across the grass like you did at West's funeral." We all started laughing but not too loud, because we were at the graveside. To make up for his joke about her, he took my mother's hand and kissed it. Then he helped her across the grass to her seat. He was such a gentleman, unlike my father, Warren.

I couldn't believe my father didn't attend the funeral. Maybe he would show his face before we left the graveside. Adrianna was like my father's twin, but she had some deep-rooted issues with him that I couldn't understand. She blamed Daddy for Mr. Donald molesting her. She felt that if Daddy hadn't left Mama when she was pregnant, she would have had a father around to protect her from the Mr. Donalds in the world. I agreed with her point, but I didn't understand the grudge. I was the first person she'd told, and I'd felt helpless. As the older sister, I always wondered why it wasn't me instead of her. I should have protected her. I had been so into the books that I hadn't kept my eye on the streets. I wished it had been me, because the abuse changed my sister forever. She had been the most loving out of all of us, and now she was the most coldhearted. Sometimes I felt she was not capable of love— until times like this. Even though she had not broken down about Boss's death, the look on her face said she was in a lot of pain. "Have you heard from Daddy?" I asked Jullian, taking a seat beside Adrianna. Mama and Joseph were seated next to her. We were all in the front row as his family because Boss hadn't kept in touch with his immediate family after his parents' death. He had known it had to be an inside job, so instead of figuring out whom he could trust, he'd decided to trust no one.

Trying to whisper, Jullian said, "Adrianna told him that if his presence didn't make a difference, then his absence wouldn't matter. You know she can be so cutthroat sometimes." I looked at her with a blank stare, because on a bad day, Jullian could be just as cutthroat as Adrianna.

I gave her a warm smile and asked, "How are you holding up, Sis? Between yesterday and today, I know you are drained." I took her hand.

"Charisma, you have always been my rock. I miss West so much. I couldn't stop crying last night, but I'm good now. Not only that—do you see that white cracker over there, leaning against that black Charger?"

"Why does he have to be a cracker? But okay, who is it?" I said, rolling my eyes to show disgust at her racial statement. Ever since she'd found out that her first boyfriend was cheating on her with a white girl, she had been prejudiced from that day forward.

"That's the detective that has been asking me one hundred and one questions about West and Bossman's murder."

"Huh! Adrianna didn't tell me that the detectives were questioning you too," I said without trying to raise my voice. Everyone was there now. I knew the preacher was about to start soon, so I tried to talk as fast as I could.

Jullian looked at me as if she were surprised and said, "I don't know why you don't know, because Darnelle does. He is representing her regarding her involvement with West's case." Before I could respond, the pastor started the graveside service.

The service was beautiful, especially the part when seven white doves were released at the end. Seven was a symbol of completion. West had been a Shemar Moore lookalike, and Boss had practically been Rick Ross's twin. When I was looking around for my daddy, I saw the detective taking pictures from his car. I gave him an evil look. He paused for a minute when he saw my face but then started photographing again. He was tall, had salt-and-pepper hair and dark eyes, and was sexy like George Clooney. I looked around for my daddy again. I guessed he had taken Adrianna's word at face value when she'd told him not to attend, just as he'd taken my mother's word when she'd told him she didn't want him anymore.

He left my mother when she was pregnant with Adrianna after they had an argument over Ms. Beverly being pregnant with Jullian at the same time. He knew my mother still wanted to be with him. He knew she was just mad and hurt that he had not only cheated but also not used protection and then gotten someone pregnant. He used leaving as an excuse to get away from seeing the pain in her eyes. He was weak. A real man would have stayed with the woman he loved to make things better. She was his wife, not just some girlfriend. You couldn't spill milk and expect it not to spoil. You cleaned it up immediately, or you would just make matters worse. Instead, he decided to pour himself another glass of milk—Ms. Beverly—and left my mother and his relationship on the floor to spoil. He found out karma could be a bitch unless you treated her right.

Ms. Beverly played her hand well for the first year or so, thinking she could change my father. They had threesomes and were swingers with some of their friends. They even once tried to pull a stripper from Onyx, Charlotte's most profitable strip club. She thought as long as she fed him and sexed him, she could get him to wife her. She was wrong. My father still loved my mother, but once he walked out that door and into Ms. Beverly's arms, he knew it would be hard to come back home. When Beverly saw that Daddy was never going to file for divorce, stop cheating, or marry her no matter what she did, she went insane. Her family had to seek help for her when she tried to commit suicide for the second time after she caught my father cheating on her. I couldn't feel sorry for Daddy, because he knew she was crazy when he met her. He told himself that her problem was just insecurity, but word on the street was that everyone knew it was much more than that. She had a past of cutting men, lying about being abused to the police in order to get men arrested for cheating on her, damaging cars, and breaking into their other women's houses. My grandfather always said, "Never play with a heart that is already broken, especially if a broken mind comes with it." My mama never looked back, even though her heart was broken. She said she prayed, and God told her to release him, so that was what she did. She said if God told her to do anything different, then she would do that as well, but until then, Mama kept it moving.

A few months later, while still pregnant with Adrianna, she started dating her ob-gyn, Dr. Joseph C. James. Joseph and my mother had been together ever since. He had proposed to her twice. He was so in love that he'd never once figured that Mama was still married to my daddy. They'd never gotten a divorce. I asked my mama why she hadn't told him. Her reply was "He never asked, so I never told him."

The funeral was over, and I couldn't wait to get out of there. My stomach was still in knots. "Come on, baby—let me get you home," Darnelle said, helping me stand up and looking at me with a smile. He had the most hypnotizing eyes. After I told Adrianna that she could stay with me as long as she wanted, Darnelle chimed in. "Anything you need, just ask." Then he leaned in and whispered into her ear, "Come by my office first thing Monday morning. We need to get your affairs together before Detective Clark over there does it for you."

She nodded in agreement, and then he kissed her on her forehead to say good-bye. She told me she loved me, as she always did after our sisterly conversations, and we hugged. Then Darnelle took me home so that I could lie down.

CHAPTER 3

·············· ⚬⚬⚬ ··············

Jullian

I cried so much at West's funeral yesterday that I said to myself, "I'll be damned if I drop a tear today. Plus, Adrianna needs me to be the strong one for her today, like she was for me at my man's funeral yesterday." I was mad as fuck that I hadn't eaten that morning, because I could tell we were going to start late. I told Adrianna she should have used Paul Mitchell's funeral services, which we'd used for West, but no—this hoe just had to use a BOB. That means "black-owned business." Every person dealing with a BOB should be prepared for possible bullshit to happen at any given time.

So now I was hungry, and I had just started my cycle that morning. Knowing that the first day was the heaviest day, could you imagine my face when I remembered that morning that Boss had requested everyone wear all white? I threw my hands up over my head and accidentally said aloud, "This nigga!" in disgust.

Everyone was downstairs in the foyer and living room, waiting for others and the funeral-home limos to arrive. I noticed Dream reading her Bible, preparing for her closing prayer. She looked just like Charisma and Adrianna but mostly Charisma. If I wasn't in the family, you couldn't have paid me to believe that Dream was adopted. Auntie Diane did a great job with her. Aunt Diane couldn't have any kids, so adopting Dream had been heaven to her.

Adrianna insisted on driving her own vehicle for whatever reason. All of the men in the family offered to drive her, but she refused them respectfully. She wouldn't even let anyone ride with her. I figured she just needed time to be alone. Everyone handled death differently. Who was I to judge? Thank God Adrianna and Boss had a mansion just like West and I did, because I needed to use a private bathroom. I dashed off to look for one upstairs. Adrianna and I lived on two different sides of town in order to give each other space. She lived in the Ballantyne community, not far from *American Idol* winner and singer Fantasia. West and I had a mansion in South Park, near South Park Mall. Ballantyne was new money, and a lot of the celebrities stayed there. South Park was old money, and people who made and invested in the celebrities stayed there. Just about everything in Ballantyne was new. South Park had been around for years and had a mixture of old and new multimillion-dollar homes. West and I were blessed because our home had been a gift from his grandfather in a roundabout way. When he died, he left his home to West, his eldest grandchild. At least if the police came questioning us about anything, our home was secure. I couldn't say that about Boss and Adrianna's home.

When I got to the top of the steps, I startled the shit out of Charisma, who immediately hit the End button on her phone, hanging up on whomever she had been speaking to. "Bitch, you look guilty as hell," I said, laughing at the expression she had on her face, when she turned around after sensing someone behind her. "Move your Beyoncé ass out of the way," I said playfully, smacking her ass to get past her to go inside the hall bathroom.

"How much did you hear, Jullian?"

"Hear of what?" I asked, knowing darn well what she was referring to. I just wanted to keep her on her toes.

"Hoe, don't play with me. How much did you hear of my conversation just now?"

I laughed again because Charisma used the word *hoe* instead of *bitch*, which Adrianna and I used when referring to our sisters playfully and lovingly. Charisma didn't smoke, drink, or curse and was still a virgin. I sometimes wondered, *Are they sure we came out of the same coochie? Are they sure Maury isn't going to say, "You are not the father," to our daddy one day?* If she hadn't looked just like our mother, with her pretty eyes and caramel skin, I would have written to Maury myself.

"Okay, clearly you heard something, because you're laughing and playing dumb with me, so I'm going to just fill you in. Honestly, I'm glad I can get this off my chest, because I'm tired of holding it in anyway."

I really hadn't heard anything, but Charisma wanted to spill the beans, so my ears opened. I needed some gossip in my life to distract me from West's death anyway. "Well, come in the bathroom with me, and tell me," I said, pulling my dress up after walking into the oversized bathroom. The bathroom had his and hers sinks, and it wasn't even the master bathroom. Charisma sat down at the vanity mirror and makeup section, which was trimmed in gold, and began admiring her beauty in the mirror. I couldn't lie—all of my sisters were beautiful. *If I was a nigga, they both could get it,* I thought with a slight grin. I opened up the separate bathroom door to the room that housed the toilet only. It was a Toto Aquia, dual-flush toilet with a seat warmer. You pressed button one for the number one and button two for the number two. It had been West's and my gift to Adrianna and Boss when they'd gotten their mansion built. I was a believer in giving things that people could actually use for an extended period of time. Since we had one and I was sitting on the toilet when I was thinking of a housewarming gift, the toilet it was.

"Okay, I'm listening. Get to talking before I give you my speech," I said through the door, still acting as if I'd overheard some of her conversation. I would have never imagined in my wildest dreams what that bitch told me.

Charisma began to tell me the story. "Remember I told you about the Scared Straight teen program that I'm heading up for the

Department of Juvenile Justice?" Before I could say yes, she kept on talking. "Well, I was making the final arrangements, and we begin next week. Anyway, I was exiting the courthouse and ran directly into Rashad—literally."

Shocked, I said, "*Rashad* Rashad?"

Running her fingers through her hair, she replied, "Yes, girl. *Rashad* Rashad." She smiled every time she said Rashad's name.

The day Rashad Jones's family moved, he had given Adrianna a letter to give to Charisma. My parents had refused to give him my auntie Diane's address, where Charisma was sent to live after the rape of Adrianna. Adrianna, to this day, thought no one knew that she wasn't just molested, but a mother always knew. Ms. Josephine was the mother I never had. Mothers always knew the truth. In order to protect Charisma, they'd sent her off for nine months. Mr. Donald had moved shortly after, but they'd told everyone they didn't want to interrupt Charisma's schooling, so she wouldn't be moving back until after the school year was over. Unfortunately for Charisma, the school year had just started. I'd moved in with them the summer Charisma came back home. We had been inseparable ever since.

"I didn't realize that it was him at first, because our collision made me drop my briefcase. I bent down quickly, racing to pick it up before he did, because it had confidential information in it. I got a sniff of his cologne when I was gathering his papers, and my pussy immediately got wet. Then I saw a strong, brown-skinned hand, with a wedding-ring tan around the ring finger, reach to help me up. When I looked up, he was standing so close to me, face-to-face, that I could see the juiciness of his lips outlined by a perfectly shaped goatee. I realized it was Rashad. Then, when he smiled, showing his perfectly white, pearly teeth, I think I lost my breath, girl." She fanned herself while checking her phone to see if my mother had called to tell us the limo had arrived. She hadn't called, so Charisma continued. "Of course, he looked like he just left a *GQ* magazine shoot with his black Armani suit that hung so well. He asked me to walk with him around the corner, so I did. Of course, he let me lead. I had to put my Lisa Raye swag on because I knew that he would be watching me in my tailor-made, fitted navy-blue pin-striped suit and navy-blue pumps that were professional but sexy.

"As soon as we got around the corner, he pinned me against the wall with his body. All I could hear was the music of water from the waterfall that ran off the side of the courthouse building. I immediately felt his nature rise and the sexual tension that filled the air when he looked into my eyes."

"Oh shit! Did you grab it?" I said, being freaky.

"No, I didn't grab it."

"Bitch, you stupid. I would have grabbed it, and if no one was looking, I might have teased it with my tongue at least once. You know I like to put on a show." We both laughed.

"Jullian, you have always been the freak of the family."

I clapped my hands and said, "And proud of it."

"Just before we kissed, my phone rang."

"Damn, girl, you know how to fuck up a wet dream, don't you? If I wasn't on my cycle, I would have probably been playing with myself under my skirt in here while you are telling me the story."

We started cracking up, and then she continued. "It was the jailhouse ring, so I had to answer it, Jullian. Judge Richard Ross is a hard-ass, and he has no problem embarrassing people in the courtroom, especially woman. It's like he has something against women, even though he is married to North Carolina senator, Senator Mary C. Ross, a Charlotte native. You can tell he didn't have a good relationship with his mother," she said sarcastically. "So I told Rashad I had to go. He looked down at my left hand and saw my engagement ring. Sadness crept into his eyes. I wanted to snatch my hand away, because it reminded me that I was engaged as well. The moment I saw him, I forgot who I was, and I wanted to keep it that way. He said that he had to file some paperwork at the courthouse but had to see me, even if it was one last time."

"So what did you say?" I said, trying to speak over the water she ran to wash her hands.

"I said yes. We are meeting at South Park Marriott next week during lunch."

"Bitch, if you wasn't engaged and waiting to lose your virginity on your wedding night, I would tell you to give that nigga some! You just have to be a virgin," I said, playfully rolling my eyes.

I heard her grab the doorknob to leave. Then I heard her say with a smile in her voice, "That's the thing. I'm not." The door closed.

I was left there speechless, but before I could get my thoughts together, my mother came in twenty seconds later. Clearly, she didn't know anyone was in the bathroom, because she had her phone on speaker. I was about to tell her I was in there, but I realized the man's voice on the other end was my father. *What the fuck do they have to talk about?* I thought.

"No, I haven't told the girls. I told you that I was going to let you tell them in your own time. Adrianna and Charisma are going through so much right now. I'm afraid one more piece of bad news would send them right over the edge, especially Jullian. I'm not so worried about Adrianna, because she hasn't even dropped a tear so far," my mother said, placing the phone on the counter.

Through the speakerphone, I heard my father say, "Adrianna is Ford tough like her father but sexy like her mother." He was trying to flirt with my mother. "I wish you would consider what I asked you, Josephine. I've been asking you for another chance since before my situation changed. Don't let us end like this. I miss you, Jo. I love you."

What in the world is going on? I said to myself, trying not to move an inch on the toilet. *Did my father just tell my mother that he loves her? When did they start speaking again? Did they ever really stop? Isn't he with Chantal?* My mind was already reeling from Charisma telling me about her and Rashad, and now my mother and father seemed as if they had their own secrets as well.

"Well, you should have thought about love when we were together, Warren. I'm not going to leave Joseph for you, sick or not."

Wait—did she just say "sick"? I said to myself, trying not to even breathe too hard.

I could never be fucked up in the head like Beverly. I called her Beverly even though she was my birth mom, because at the end of the day, Josephine was my mother at heart. Beverly and my mother had been best friends for years. Just like my sisters and I, they had an "I don't do other bitches" mentality. They chose to hang out with only each other. That kept "he said, she said" drama down, because the only people they spoke to was one another. That was where my sisters and I got our attitudes from. We only dealt with one another on a personal level. Adrianna didn't give a fuck about the next bitch, because she thought she was the baddest bitch. Because of Charisma's profession, she limited who was in her circle. She worked with criminals all day, so in her head, everyone was suspect. Then there was me. I followed suit because that was how my sisters were. So far, it had worked up until recently, because for the life of me, I couldn't understand why Charisma didn't know that Adrianna's case was being handled by her fiancé. Maybe Adrianna thought Darnelle had told her and Darnelle thought Adrianna had told her. So much had been going on with the deaths of West and Bossman that everything had gotten all turned upside down. We were ride or die for one another at the end of the day, and that was all that mattered. Our motto was "Sisters forever," because you couldn't trust females—period. To confirm that, I just had to look at my mother and Beverly. They had done everything together— even my father, obviously.

Diamond was taking all of this hard. Yesterday's funeral for West had been a blur to me, so I hadn't paid much attention to her then, but today, since she was by herself, I decided to sit with her. My entire family was in attendance to support one another, because the Banks family was Bossman's only family. I was blessed to have the Styles family in my life to help with their son's funeral. To know I would never carry that last name killed me inside. Every time the wind blew, I thought it was West's way of telling me he loved me. I was surrounded by my family, but because this was Adrianna's day, and rightly so, I felt alone. Since Diamond was solo and I felt solo, I figured we might as well be together in church.

I'd always known she was pretty, but I'd never realized how gorgeous she was before today. Even with tears streaming down her face, she was a ten in every area, down to her sense of style. Since my sisters and I were always the Kardashians of the party, none of the other women in the room mattered. Also, West had gone above and beyond to make me feel as if I were the only beautiful woman in the world. I had loved him. I still did. I gathered strength, helping Diamond by rubbing her back, getting her tissues, and helping her stand to go view Bossman's body in the casket.

At least I'm doing something helpful, I thought to myself. *Anything but listening to Pastor Allen preach about himself and how he used to be in the world but now is saved—at someone else's funeral!* I was glad Pastor Barnette from House of Restoration had conducted West's funeral. For a moment, it seemed Pastor Allen forget he was at a funeral. He preached as if it were Sunday morning. *Someone should be bold enough to tell him that his Easter Sunday suit is about two sizes too small and about a decade out of style,* I thought.

After viewing Bossman, Diamond ran out of the church, crying. I was going to go after her, but she had plenty of men ready to console her and much more. I decided to go back to our seats and gather our personal belongings. When I got back to my seat, I heard her phone vibrating in her all-white Berkley purse. *Figures—she has the new iPhone.* While pressing all of the wrong buttons, I came across the surprise of my life: a picture of

Adrianna bent over a black leather sectional. She was in their media room and was wearing the sexy black-lace lingerie set I'd purchased her for her birthday last year. All I could see was wet, wavy, flowing jet-black hair and breasts perfectly held up like grapefruits by the edge of the counter. In the mirror, I could see Bossman hitting it from the back with a "Give me this pussy" expression, even with his eyes closed. Adrianna was bent over in front of the mirror, taking the picture, her breasts cupped with his big hands. The diamonds in his Gucci watch almost stole the show from the picture. *What the fuck is Diamond doing with this picture?* I thought. *Let me find out Adrianna, Boss, and Diamond were having threesomes. I thought I was the freak of the family.* I started laughing while putting the phone back into her purse, but before I did, the picture changed, and I realized that the woman in the pictures was Diamond, not Adrianna. "What the hell?" I said aloud, in the church, without realizing I'd said it at first. Thank God everyone was exiting to go to his or her car in order to drive to the grave site; however, there were a few people still lingering in the pews. The first lady of the church looked at me as if she wasn't sure what I'd just said and needed me to clarify it. I changed my facial expression, looked her right in the eye, and said, "What a tale. What a tale your husband, the pastor, gave today about his life. It was so inspirational." I knew I had her, because her face lit up, full of pride.

"Well, thank you, Ms. Jullian. Every time I hear his story from being unsaved to saved, I just thank God. I will be sure to tell him on your behalf," she said before she and the rest of church staff walked away.

I was boiling inside. Not only had Bossman been fucking this bitch, but he'd fucked the bitch in Adrianna's house. I thought to myself, *Should I just whip her ass on site? I can't tell Adrianna today out of all days.* We were in church, but right then, I didn't give a damn. This bitch had to know she had fucked with the wrong woman's man. When I got outside to hand it to her ass, everyone was already in his or her car or limo, waiting for me to get into the family car. I did, and I didn't say a word the entire ride to the grave site. The entire time, I was thinking of ways to make that bitch pay. I decided not to show out at the grave site, but that hoe had to be put on notice. I hopped out of the family limo like a jackrabbit and hurried over to Diamond, who was just about to sit down. When I handed her phone to her, she looked down at the picture on her phone. She tried to grab the phone, but I stiffly held it, looked her straight in the eyes, and said with a raised eyebrow, "Hoe, this is not over." Then I gave her a sinister half smile and sat down with my family.

CHAPTER 4

Kendra

Oh, this motherfucker thinks he is going to divorce me without a fight, huh? How dare he embarrass me, knowing I have to see those people when I'm trying cases in court? I bet everyone at my old firm is talking about me behind my back. I can't believe he used them, knowing I used to work there.

Maybe he isn't serious. Dammit, Kendra, you know he is serious. You live and die by rule number one in a divorce case. If they really want a divorce, they will get one—period. When a man is truly over his wife, he will file for divorce.

Until then, he is still married in his heart, no matter what his mouth or his temporary actions say. Shaking my head at myself, I remembered trying many cases in which the man had moved on to other women to pass time, but when it came to signing that dotted line, his heart wouldn't let him. I'd told many clients that a man would only go so far with his mind. Eventually, his heart would win in the end. His mind would allow him to pretend that it was over by dating other women, but his heart would never allow him to love them. After the lust wore off, the other women would finally realize that his heart would never belong to them. The other woman either stayed because she didn't want to hear "I told you so" from the many loved ones who'd told her to never date a married man, dying a slow death inside, or she realized that having him physically instead of emotionally, spiritually, and mentally was not worth her self-worth and got her life back. A real woman would rather be alone and happy than in a relationship and lonely. Most of the time, a woman who accepted being second string or second best normally had a broken or strained relationship with one of her parents. No matter how long she tried to hang on to him, what he did for her, or what he said to her, she could never have what rightly belonged to somebody else. Until he signed those papers, his words and temporary actions, used just to get what he wanted, meant nothing.

Looking at myself in the mirror, I started to mimic some of my coworkers in my professional white-girl voice. "I bet she was stingy with the head. I bet he'd had enough of her black-girl attitude." Still looking in the mirror, I became silent. My skin was glowing, but I wasn't glowing on the inside. I admired, just for a few seconds, how wide my hips were, spreading, giving me the shape I'd always wanted, but I couldn't even smile. Tears filled my eyes and began to drop one by one down my smooth, dark skin; across my model-high cheekbones; and down to my black Barbie-doll fitted Bebe T-shirt, where they disappeared. Then I held my stomach with my left hand, admiring the three-carat princess-cut diamond ring sparkling back at me in the gold-trimmed hallway mirror, wondering what my and Rashad's baby will look like.

I wanted to make sure my husband loved and stayed with me for me, not because I was pregnant, and that was why I refused to get off of birth control, even when he begged me to every year around the anniversary of his parents' death. I knew he was living in the moment but might regret it later. One thing I didn't want to do was be a regret again, as my twin sister, Chantal, and I were for our father. Talking to myself, in my mind, while still staring at my reflection in the mirror, I thought, *I have to have the mental satisfaction that I can keep him on my own first, even though I know having his baby will seal the deal. Rashad is a good man. After the loss of his parents, I know he wouldn't leave me with child. After all, I'm the woman he married. I'm not a baby mama. I'm not a girlfriend. I'm not just a woman he lives with to pay half of the bills. I'm his wife! He loved me enough to give me his last name. That should mean something. What should I do? Should I have the last laugh and leave him before he leaves me? Should I keep my mouth closed and just see what he does next? Maybe he won't go through with it. Maybe I should just step my game up and pour on the love like never before. Yeah, that's what I will do. I will plan a candlelight dinner just for us, throw in some Carolina Panther box tickets, and give him a mind-blowing massage with hot oil.*

I checked my phone to see what time it was. Still speaking in my head, I thought, *It's not even lunchtime yet, so I have time to go down to the Arts District on Central Avenue to get some oils, order the football tickets online, and get my vajayjay waxed at Dynasty Nails. My hair, nails, and eyebrows stay done, that saves me so much time. I love the fact that I don't have to wear weave, because my hair is long, but I don't want to sweat it out. Fuck it! I'm going all out. I need to save my marriage. The thought of his dick inside of another woman makes my head hurt. All of this anxiety is causing my chest to hurt. First, I need a thirty-minute foot massage from Andre. Yes, that will start my day off right, so my night can be right!*

Just before I made a call, my sister's shop number showed up on the caller ID. "Hi, twin! I was just about to call you to make an appointment with Andre. What's up?" I said.

"Kendra, I have so much on my mind, girl! Warren and I have been dating for six months now. You would think the motherfucker would just die already! Damn! I'm so sick of playing the 'I love you' role every night, and if that shriveled-up-balled bastard motions for me to suck his dick one more time, I swear I'm going to scream!"

Laughing, I said, "Girl, you are crazy. That's the price you pay to get paid to lay. You said he had a big dick when you first met him."

"He did before the cancer started to really get to him. He is still sexy as hell, but he can't perform. He gets all hot and bothered but can't stay up more than two minutes. That's why I keep one on the side. What's going on with you? You only call to get a massage when you are stressed. Talk to me, Sis."

I sighed before speaking, because I knew that once I started talking, I wouldn't be able to stop. I was dying to get this off of my chest. Charisma Banks. That's the problem—always has been, and looks like she always will be.

"Charisma? She doesn't seem like the type of woman that would mess with a married man. She has too much class for that, Kendra."

Rolling my eyes, I said, Bitches ain't shit! You should know, because, bitch, you're one of them.

"True, but damn, why you have to say it like that?"

"The same reason you're standing up for the woman who has my husband's heart. He finally told me that he would always love her. I said I understood because they grew up together. Then he looked at me and said, 'No, I mean I will always love her, as in, I realized I could never fully love another woman as long as she has my heart.' I didn't know if I should smack him or smack myself for thinking one day his love for her would die." Grabbing my purse from the table and heading toward the door, I stopped to look in the mirror again. I asked myself silently how I could have been so desperate and naive.

As pretty as I was, I only wanted one man: Rashad Jones. I wanted him so much that when I heard of Rashad's parents' death, I'd transferred colleges to be near him. I knew I would befriend him by relating to his loss, as Chantal and I had our own tragic story. Since he knew me from high school, it would be like second nature for us to hang out. All I had to do was ask him to help me find my way around campus. Rashad was caring, and I was so pretty that he wouldn't say no. Chantal and I were half Korean and half black. We both looked as if we could be related to Kimora Lee Simmons. We were paternal twins. Chantal wore her hair short, but I vowed to never cut mine. It hung all the way down my back, just like Kimora Lee Simmons's. Neither of us had a big booty, but our small waists and big, perky breasts made up for it.

"How would you know what she would or would not do anyway? You're not licking her!" I said angrily.

In a defensive tone, Chantal replied, "No, but that's Warren's daughter, so I have had a front-row seat for months now. First off, only hoes sleep with married men, separated or not. I should know, because I'm top-of-the-line hoe status right now. Hell, Warren is still married. Lastly, Charisma is a virgin."

My eyes popped open. Shocked, I said, "Virgin!"

"Yes, bitch, a virgin. Not a man on God's green earth has popped that cherry yet, and if Rashad had the ability to do it, he would have done it already. Clearly, that nigga didn't meet the challenge."

I remembered Rashad telling me about the time when he and Charisma had tried to make love as teens. He wasn't sure if he'd put it all the way in or not. He had become so excited that he'd cum while trying to put it in. After that bad experience, maybe she'd decided to wait. "Well, if she's not fucking my husband, she for sure is fucking him mentally, because just the other night, he told me that after all these years, he is still in love with her."

"Damn, Kendra," Chantal said while preparing dinner and sorting out Warren's medications. He was on many medications now. She made sure she gave him the right dosage with his morning protein shakes most of the time. The other times, she gave him enough to have blackouts so that she could spend his money and make him think he had done it. He thought the stress of keeping his illness from his family was causing the blackouts, but it was Chantal. Everyone still seemed to think that Daddy was Superman, but he wasn't.

Chantal knew that no one was double-checking Warren's affairs. Everyone assumed they were all lined up. She had access to everything, and she paid herself every week as if he were her weekly client. She thought to herself, *That will be one grand,* every time she had to put his balls in her mouth. He told her no one knew exactly how much money he had. He had everything on automatic draft, so he never worried about his account. He had no idea that Chantal had created an online bank account and was paying herself weekly via his account. It didn't raise a flag for the bank, because he always made payments to her place of business. She had it made for now. She hadn't built up enough courage yet to kill him quickly via an overdose in his morning shakes. If he would just die, she could withdraw everything. He wasn't depressed enough for anyone to think he would commit suicide, so that was out. Plus, the family didn't know about his illness yet. Since he was in bad shape, she decided to just let nature take its course. Warren was the chief of surgery at Presby Hospital but had taken a leave of absence. The hospital was where he'd met his wife, Josephine. They'd played doctor and nurse at work and in the bedroom.

Counting his pills out, Chantal had a flashback to how they'd first met. Chantal was sixteen years younger than Warren. She'd always loved older men. He had come in to 'Relax Your Mind' for a massage a year ago, complaining about muscle aches. He'd thought it came from stress on the job. A month later, he'd found out he had bone cancer. He'd asked for the best via phone, and of course, as the owner, Chantal had told him she was the best. Chantal had seen a future with him when they first met. She liked all of his children, especially Jullian, whom she saw the most. He was every woman's dream; he was a doctor and a tall, light-skinned, handsome older gentleman with green eyes. He'd even taught her some new tricks in the bedroom. However, too many secrets had caused her heart to turn cold.

First, she found out he was still married to Josephine and had no intention of telling her. That meant to her that he had no intention of a future with her. He was with her to pass time. He acted as if he hated Josephine, but every time he said her name with a straight face, his eyes told another story. The icing on the cake was when she found out that he'd told Josephine about his cancer first. The cherry on top was that instead of asking Chantal to go to his chemo treatments with him, he asked Josephine. He tried to say he asked her because Josephine was a nurse and because he didn't want to stress Chantal out. She knew there was more to the story. Anytime a man left a woman out in a crisis, that meant he still had feelings for someone else. He let her in but not all the way in. Chantal realized that even though he was fond of her and she had him physically, she would never have him emotionally. He would never give her his entire heart, and a part of it was not enough for her. So when Kendra told her that Rashad was still in love with Charisma, she understood the pain a little bit, because Warren was still in love with his wife. Chantal felt there was no way in hell that her situation could be as painful as Kendra's, because Kendra was married to the man. However, it was still painful, so in order to guard her heart, she ripped it out. If Warren wanted to use her for sex and her time, then she would use him for his time and money until death did them part.

Chantal sat on the phone and listened to Kendra go on and on about her and Rashad's marital issues, but after her sister told her that Rashad was still in love with Charisma, she couldn't help but reflect silently on her relationship with Warren. The entire time Kendra was cursing Charisma out on the phone, saying things Chantal knew Kendra wouldn't say to Charisma's face, Chantal could sense Kendra getting angrier by the minute. "I'm turning onto Fairview Road now, so I will be there in less than five minutes," Kendra said.

Chantal snapped back to the conversation when she heard Andre's name, and she said, "And I already know to have you a chill glass of peach Cîroc ready."

Kendra said with a smile, "Not this time, Sis. I was going to wait until I saw you, but you are going to be an auntie. I'm three months pregnant!"

"Pregnant!" Chantal screamed with joy through her office phone.

Passing South Park Mall in her Range Rover, Kendra drifted off while driving, daydreaming about all of the shopping sprees she and her sister would have while shopping for the baby. However, before she could rejoice with her sister, *boom*. She ran a red light and T-boned an ambulance that was leaving a hotel parking lot with flashing lights.

Chapter 5

Charisma

Charisma looked around the hotel lobby to see if anyone she knew was there. After all, she knew a lot of people in the Queen City, because she was a federal probation officer. She felt dirty but excited to meet Rashad. The week of waiting had seemed like the longest week ever. Attending the funerals and planning the wedding at the same time was exhausting. She wouldn't dare complain, because it could have been her man who was killed. She loved Darnelle, but today she was going to find out once and for all if another man held the key to her heart. In the elevator, going up to the eleventh floor, she heard one of R&B singer Fantasia's songs playing: "Truth is, I never got over you. Truth is ..." Right before she got off the elevator, she thought, *What if Kendra found out I met her husband? She would automatically assume that we are fucking. Kendra would probably sue me like Paula Cook sued Fantasia, and Kendra is a lawyer—a divorce lawyer at that!*

When the elevator doors opened, she saw Judge Richard Ross and an unknown male standing in front of her. They were waiting to get into the elevator. She immediately felt guilt, as if the judge could read her mind and knew why she was there. She closed her eyes and looked down for a second in shame, but when she opened them and lifted her head, she noticed that Judge Ross and the unknown man were holding hands. He had forgotten they were holding hands. When he noticed her, he immediately pushed the hand of his partner away.

"Good afternoon, Judge Ross," Charisma said with a slight grin. Her eyes said, "You know you're as good as caught with your bitch ass, don't you?"

"Good afternoon, Ms. Banks," he said, tilting his head as if he had respect for her as a lady.

Charisma exited the elevator, laughing on the inside, and looked for room 1105. Before she could knock, the door opened. Rashad handed her some papers and said, "All week long, I've been trying to find the right way to tell you, but I couldn't find the words, so I decided to just show you. You always told me, Charisma, that my actions should be so apparent that my words shouldn't even matter. Open it," he said in his baritone voice.

She heard what he said, but he looked so sexy in his Marc Jacobs dress shirt, slacks, and tie and smelled so good that she lost her train of thought. He was six foot three, brown skinned, slanted eyes, a bald head, a clean-shaven face, long, thick eyelashes, and a perfect smile. Noticing his big dick imprint, she couldn't even think straight.

"Come over to the bed and let me take your shoes off," he said. He motioned her over to the bed and began removing her caramel Prada heels. She still couldn't open her mouth; she had no words. He began to massage her feet after he placed the papers on her lap, waiting for her to open them.

"Ah, that feels so good, Rashad," she finally said with a groan. She grabbed the papers, looked at them, and realized they were divorce papers. "Oh my God! You filed for divorce?"

He smiled and replied, "I just couldn't do it anymore, baby. I don't want to hurt Kendra, so the moment I realized the truth, I had to tell her the truth."

Charisma smiled and asked, "What is the truth?"

Placing her right foot to the side, he slid in between her legs, looked her right in the eyes, and said, "The moment I found an old picture of you and I cuddled up at the state fair in my old college box, I knew. It just hit me like a ton of bricks. From that day forward, I never went a day without thinking about you. I told myself to wait at least thirty days, and if I felt the same way, then I had to admit it to myself first and then to my wife. The day I ran into you at the courthouse, I was there to file and to find you." He passed her a glass of champagne with strawberries in it.

"To see me?" she asked, surprised.

"Yes, to see you. I looked you up on day twenty-nine, when I realized that day thirty was approaching. I found out that you were a probation officer, and not only that, you were engaged," he said somberly. "I was going to go to your office and leave a note, but I literally ran right into you. I knew then it was meant to be." He started whispering, "I knew it was meant to be," over and over again as he leaned closer and closer to her full lips glossed with Victoria's Secret strawberry lip gloss.

The entire time, she was thinking, *This isn't right. He is a married man. I'm about to be a married woman.* He slid his hand up her dress and began to massage her clit. Then he placed his thumb on her clit as he inserted his long middle finger into her sweet peach. *What is this man doing to me? I can't sleep with him after I told Darnelle that he would be the only one. The thought of my first time with Darnelle didn't get me this excited, and that is why it was our last time. I always thought love and the blessing of marriage would handle the rest in time, but Rashad is making me lose my mind!* she thought. Slowly moving in and out with his right hand, he unbuttoned the top of her white dress, with his left hand, exposing her white Victoria's Secret bra, which held her grapefruit-like breasts perfectly. Right before she creamed, he bent down, licked, and sucked her until he tasted her pineapple cum all over his lips. Seeing that, Charisma said the words she was supposed to say on her wedding night. Seductively, she said, "Put it in." Rashad was so excited that precum was leaking from his swollen, perfectly shaped head. His mind was racing because he had never cheated on his wife.

As a celebrity real-estate broker, he'd had numerous opportunities, but he had never wanted to cheat. It wasn't worth it to him in the long run, and Rashad always thought things out before acting. He told himself that if he was consistent in his feelings for thirty days straight, then his feelings weren't just a phase. He lived and died by that rule. He and Kendra had separated before for twenty-one days, and he'd never seen another woman. He'd buried himself in work and hadn't even allowed himself to touch Kendra anymore, fearing he would be drawn back in. He had been mean to her on purpose just to push her away, because he'd needed time to think. He'd wanted to know if his marriage was a mistake. He'd never had a chance to complete the thirty-day trial, however, because Kendra's suicide attempt had caused him to go back home. Since he still loved his wife and she wasn't a bad person, leaving her wasn't worth her taking her life, especially because he wasn't sure if leaving was what he wanted to do. She would have taken her life for nothing.

He couldn't have that on his head. However, the thought of what his wife had done to him during the separation made it easier for him to be with Charisma right now.

One night, he'd come home and found she wasn't home yet. He'd waited for her by the fireplace with soft throw pillows, a lit fire, chocolate-covered strawberries, wine, and Luther Vandross softly playing in the air. He had fallen asleep waiting, but he'd awakened to laughter on his front porch at two o'clock in the morning. He'd grabbed his nine from the fireplace mantel and peeked out the side window at the front door. Sliding the curtain back, he had seen an unidentified man helping his wife stand up while trying to pull her keys out at the same time. Rashad had been about to open the door, but then he'd thought if he did, he would never know the truth. With his Escalade parked in the garage, she hadn't even known he was home. "Thank you for the coffee and bringing me home, Martin," she'd said.

Martin! From the law firm? Oh, hell no! he'd thought to himself, but he'd refused to blow his cover yet.

Pulling her deep red Juicy Couture dress down, trying to stand up, she'd softly kissed him on his cheek and said, "Goodnight."

As she had gone to turn the doorknob, he'd gently grabbed her and said, "Can I smell it again?"

Rashad had pulled open the door, pointed his steel directly at Martin's head in a fit of rage, and said, "No, but you can feel this bullet if you don't get the hell off of my wife!"

Martin had taken off running like a track star to his silver Mercedes coupe with custom-made rims. Rashad had shot one time in the air for kicks. Hearing that gunshot had caused Martin to dive headfirst, like Olympic swimmer Michael Phelps, through the passenger-side window of the car and speed off. Rashad had been furious, but the moment he'd looked at Kendra, his anger had gone away. Kendra had never had alcohol before. He had seen that she was drunk for the first time ever in her life. She hadn't even flinched when he'd shot up into the air, so he'd known she was gone like two sheets to the wind. He'd removed her soaked panties; placed her in the shower; washed her hair, which smelled like alcohol; rubbed her with her favorite lotion; and then laid her down in front of the fireplace and held her all night. The next morning, she hadn't even remembered what had happened. Since she hadn't remembered it, he'd buried it. He'd figured he would give her a pass for getting her pussy eaten out by another man, since he had left her and she had been drunk. As much as it hurt him to be quiet about that night, he'd known that if he hadn't left, that night would never have happened. Two months later, he'd decided to let go of anything that would hinder his future with his wife, so he'd started throwing out his hidden stash of pictures and letters from old sweethearts. When he had run across Charisma and his picture of her, he had been shocked. He'd thought he'd burned all of their pictures, especially the good-bye letter he'd received from her, ending their relationship when she left with her aunt. He was so hurt about their breakup that he never wanted to see her face again. Seeing that picture of them, with her wearing his college football jacket while he held her at the fair, the two of them smiling as if they had no worries in the world, had melted his heart. He had fallen in love all over again. No matter how many other women he had loved and how much he loved his wife, he had only been in love once, and that was with Charisma Banks. He'd decided to follow his thirty-day rule that day. When he'd filed for divorce, he'd felt free to do whatever he liked for the first time.

"Are you sure you want me to put it in?" Rashad said in his sexy voice. His mind was racing because he respected the fact that Charisma was a virgin. He wanted it, but he wanted her to want it, and he wanted it to be right. His intentions had been to get her all hot and bothered and just enjoy the tease. He had never imagined she would give him permission to go all the way to home base. He was so hard, and he was letting his shaft slide up and down her, teasing her and himself.

Then a flashback crossed his mind of the two of them back in high school, two months before they broke up. She had given him permission to put it in then. He had been a virgin and hadn't known what he was doing. He'd thought he had it in but hadn't been sure. He hadn't been sure if she was squirming because he was in or because she was nervous with the anticipation of him going all the way in. He'd had precum leaking in his excitement. The excitement of her letting him go all the way and of him trying to pop her cherry had become too much, and he'd cum all over her. He had been embarrassed. They'd decided to wait until they got married and had never tried again. Shortly after, about two months later, she'd broken up with him, when her mother had sent her to live with her aunt Diane. Rashad had been heartbroken to no end. He'd vowed to never fall in love again.

"We can't do this, Charisma."

She sat up and said, "Why not?" She felt relieved, angered, and rejected at the same time.

"Even though I moved out this morning, Kendra is still my wife, and I'm still her husband. You deserve better than this."

Hearing those words—"you deserve better than this"—took her back to the day Adrianna had mailed her Rashad's good-bye letter with those exact same words. Charisma jumped up and started buttoning her blouse as fast as she could. "I can't believe you came back into my life just to tease me, fill my head with 'I love you' lies, and then leave me again!" she yelled, grabbing her shoes and walking toward the door to leave.

Rashad was taken aback because he had no idea what had set her off. He was trying to tell her that he wanted to wait to make love to her because she deserved to have her first time be special. He didn't want her to be a mistress. He wanted her to be his wife. Before he could get that thought out of his mouth, Charisma was gone.

I can't believe I let myself get weak for him again, she thought. *I always vowed that I would let myself love but never fall in love with a man ever again. Now here I am, looking stupid. I can't let him hurt me again. I have a good man waiting to marry me. This is what I get for coming here in the first place.* She hurried out of the lobby. *Shit, I didn't realize it is almost one o'clock. I have to get back to court.* Rushing out of the hotel, she cut through the grass instead of using the sidewalk.

Boom! She fell and twisted her ankle. She was almost to her car, so she hopped to the row where her car was parked. Her ankle was in pain. She wanted to call Rashad to come help her, but she didn't have time to deal with him. She held on to the trunk flap of a pickup truck and bent over to take her heel off. The driver of the truck didn't see her behind him, because he was arguing with his wife about being late to pick her up. In a rush, he forcibly backed up right into Charisma, knocking her over. She fell unconscious. When the ambulance came, Rashad was walking to his car. He saw that Charisma had been hit, rushed immediately to her side, and jumped into the ambulance with her. "I love you, Charisma. Please don't leave me again. I just found you," he said holding her hand, tears falling from his face. *Boom!* A woman driving a silver Range Rover ran a red light and T-boned the ambulance.

CHAPTER 6

<hr/>

Adrianna

As soon as I got off of the elevator, I heard, "Adrianna Banks is here to see you, sir." The receptionist spoke with a fake professional voice.

I said to myself as I walked right past her with an "I don't need permission to enter" attitude, "This bitch must not know who I am, because Adrianna Banks doesn't need an introduction." As soon as I entered, he leaned back in his chair behind his desk, meaning he wanted me to come over to him. I decided to tease him first by standing in my sexy diva pose while slowly untying my valentine-red MK trench coat until

I was standing in my six-inch heels and wearing nothing else. My eyes told him I wanted him. His eyes and the licking of his lips told me he wanted me more. I knew the drill. This wasn't the first time, but it was the first time during business hours. The mere thought of me secretly fucking him on the twenty-third floor, looking over downtown Charlotte, with other people in the building made my panties wet. I walked over to him and, never losing eye contact, dropped my coat. Then I placed an envelope on his desk. "Open when I say to" was written on the front of the envelope. I straddled him. He was already up and ready for Ms. Kitty. He smelled good. I could have licked his asshole and his balls at the same damn time. "Bitch, you know you want this dick," he said, grabbing my ass with his masculine hands as I unbuttoned his shirt. I grabbed my breasts with both hands, and then I started licking my left nipple to tease him even more. He loved that shit—that did it for him every time. He slid me onto Mr. Hardknock, and right before I reached heaven, his secretary came on his emergency speaker.

In a panic, she said, "Mr. Mitchell, Presby Hospital is on the phone stating that Ms. Banks had an accident and was just transported to the hospital."

Darnelle and I immediately jumped up and were on our way to the hospital.

When we arrived, he flew past me and started running down the hallway to the emergency-room desk. The staff rushed him to the back. He was in such a hurry that he didn't even see Jullian in the waiting room. Charisma was bruised and sore but had no broken bones. Mama was in the back with Charisma, and Daddy and Chantal were on the way. Only two visitors could see her at a time. "I just came out to try to call you, because there isn't any signal back there," Jullian said. After Jullian told me what had happened, I felt relieved. Although I was fucking my sister's man, I would have hated for something serious to happen to her, knowing I was on his dick. After all, she was my sister.

After about ten minutes, I said, "I'm going to go back there to swap with Mama." Since Darnelle had just gotten there, I knew he wasn't leaving her side.

When I got up, Jullian asked, "Why are you rocking a trench in September? It's chilly in the morning but not that chilly. We are still wearing sandals. Let me find out."

I couldn't help but laugh because she was looking at me suspiciously. "I just jumped up and threw on the first thing I found when we got the call."

"We? Who the fuck is we?" she asked, playing detective.

"I meant as soon as I got the call, Jullian. I'll be right back. Let me go check on Sis," I said, hurrying out of the waiting room and down the hall. I hated hiding things from her. She let it go because she figured if I'd wanted her to know, I would have just told her. I loved that about her.

She never started trouble, but if pushed too hard, she would finish it.

As I was walking down the hall, to my surprise, I saw Diamond's brother, Sly, walking into the hospital. I decided to follow him past the emergency room's waiting room to the main elevators. I stood behind a huge plant, waiting for him to get on the elevator. When he did, I watched the elevator light go to the sixth floor. The only reason I didn't call the police was because I wanted to body-bag him myself. I was waiting for events to die down before I did it. Officer Styles was watching my every move, because he thought I knew more than I did about West's and Bossman's deaths. He'd even alluded to the fact that I might have set my own people up. He needed to find something else better to do with his life and stay out of mine. I was outside in the car when Bossman and West were killed. All I saw was a black van pull up and leave five minutes later. I assumed it was a drop, but when Boss didn't answer his phone or come out ten minutes after the van left, I went inside the safe house. The killers used silencers, and if Bossman's truck didn't have illegal tint, I probably would have been dead as well. Thank the Lord he didn't take it off even after getting two illegal-tint tickets for it.

When I got to the sixth floor, I heard a ring tone: "Gangsta Music" by Jeezy. I followed the ring, and then I saw Sly leaving a room, talking on his cell phone, going down the hall in the opposite direction. His Brooklyn accent caught my attention. It was sexy. If I hadn't known him, overhearing his conversation would have turned me on. I would have immediately known he was from the streets. I had a thing for street niggas, but corner boys were a turnoff. I didn't do up-and-coming dope boys. My man definitely already had to be a boss.

Sly's back was against the wall, and he had one leg up. He was moving his hands to express his point. "Yeah, man, Dia won't give me the green light, but I'm about to green-light this hit myself," he said at normal volume.

That type of foolishness was why I could never respect a corner boy like him. Only someone green would speak on the phone at a normal volume and, worse yet, with his back turned to an open entrance. I could have been the police— or me. I looked into the room he was coming out of, and to my surprise, Diamond was in the hospital bed inside the room. Now I knew that when Sly had said "Dia," he had been referring to Diamond. I immediately became enraged all over again. She was sleeping, looking like a black Sleeping Beauty. Even when she was asleep, she was gorgeous. I quickly closed the blue curtain behind me. I wondered if Charisma had her gun with her in the ER. Since she was a probation officer, she always carried her gun. I decided I should go back downstairs to get it but changed my mind when I remembered that Charisma's gun didn't have a silencer on it. So I stood over her and grabbed the pillow from behind her head. "Bitch, you don't need this, do you?" I said, and I started smothering her with the pillow.

She started to fight back, but I could tell her body was weak from her injuries. Then it crossed my mind that she was in the hospital because of our fight. I came to the realization that the reason she hadn't called the police was because she was going to seek revenge. That angered me even more, so I started to push down harder. "Die, bitch," I said. As I was holding the pillow down, I started thinking about all of the times she and Boss had fucked in my house, all of the late-night phone calls, and all of the laughs they'd had at my expense. Then, out of nowhere, I felt someone grab me. It was Darnelle.

"Adrianna, what in the world are you doing?" he said, sitting Diamond up to catch her breath.

"What does it look like I'm doing, Darnelle?" I said with an attitude.

"Bitch, you are crazy!" he said, shaking his head. "I just got word from my police department connection that Diamond was in the hospital. I came to talk to her to see if she had any information that could help clear your name. Well, you fucked that up, now, didn't you, Adrianna?"

I sighed. Diamond, trying to catch her breath, asked for some water from her nightstand. Darnelle gladly helped her sip some water out of her straw, as if he were used to it. I saw him admiring her beauty as she sucked the straw. I shot him a look that said, "Don't make me fuck you up." At that point, I noticed she had a mark on her head from a head bandage, which she'd likely needed because I'd hit her in the head with that graveside shovel.

She looked at me and said, "No one knows Bossman's and West's grind better than you and I, and every day we are at odds, we are losing money on the streets. With that being said, I need you, and you most definitely need me. So are you ready to make this money, or are you ready to be buried with none of it?"

I was taken aback at her boss-like attitude. I was turned on more than angry now. A voice in the back of my mind was saying, *Bitch, you are tripping. Don't lay down with the enemy.*

She saw that I was shocked by her reaction, but she made her case with confidence anyway. I knew then why Boss and West had chosen her. "Either way, business must go on, and money needs to be made."

I thought for a few seconds about what she was asking me, because I was in shock. Had she forgotten that I'd just tried to take her out? I could tell she knew I was going to say yes, but it was going to take me a minute or so to process her proposal. I felt uncomfortable that she could read me. She continued, saying, "Yeah, I fucked your man. So what? It was just sex and fun times. You are the one who had his heart and was about to get the ring. I'm wrong, and you're right. That's why I couldn't even green-light the hit on you."

I came out of my state of shock and, with a stone-cold face, gave her a look that said, "Bitch, I'm not ever scared."

The look didn't move her, or at least she pretended that it didn't move her. Either way, she knew it was real. She said, "At the end of the day, Boss loved himself more than any of us. Can we move on now?"

I had no love for the hoe, but she was speaking my language. I took a deep breath and looked at the seriousness in her eyes. I pulled up a chair beside her bed, and then I asked Darnelle to leave the room. Diamond and I had business to discuss.

CHAPTER 7

Kendra

Every time I opened my eyes, either Chantal or Rashad was there. Rashad kept going in and out of the hospital room, but I was too weak to worry about why. I just needed to know about my baby and whether anyone else was hurt.

"Hi, Sis. Rashad stepped out but will be right back. How are you feeling?" Chantal asked, looking at me with concern in her eyes.

I didn't utter a word at first. My mind was still racing about what had happened. I knew that some people who got into accidents didn't remember anything, but not me. Unfortunately, I remembered running the red light and hitting the ambulance, and so would my insurance company. "Baby … hurt?" was all I could muster to say.

"Let me get Rashad for you, Kendra."

I grabbed her arm as she was turning to leave me and gave her a look that said, "Just tell me."

"I'm sorry, Sis," Chantal said. "The baby didn't make it."

I began to cry in silence. Her eyes showed me she was sad that I was sad, but it seemed she also had something else to tell me as soon as my loss of the baby sank in. I thought to myself, *Well, everything happens for a reason. Rashad left me anyway, and maybe this was best. I just don't know what to think right now.*

Chantal interrupted my thoughts, saying, "Only one other person was hurt, but she is okay. She only had minor injuries." Then, with a firm but sarcastic tone and tight lips, she said, "Trust me—she won't press charges."

I could hear Rashad, Warren, and some ladies talking in the hallway. Chantal went out into to hallway like a hawk to see who the nice-looking woman talking to her man, Warren, was. "Hi. My name is Chantal, and you are?" she said, grabbing Warren's hand with her left hand and extending her right to the beautiful lady. I turned the volume on the hospital TV down so that I could hear what was going on. If there was going to be a fight, at least I could forget about my tragedy for a few minutes.

Warren cut in quickly and said, "This is Josephine's sister, Diane, and Diane's daughter, Dream." When Chantal realized Diane was not going to extend her hand, she took hers back and placed it on Warren's chest. That was funny to me, because Chantal was not even thinking about Warren anymore. She just didn't want anyone else to have him. As a matter of fact, I could tell she was interested in someone else. She just wasn't ready to discuss it yet, which was cool. She would eventually tell me. I was her twin sister.

"You look just like Josephine from a distance. I thought you were her twin, like my sister and

I," Chantal said with a smile, trying to soften the atmosphere now that she knew Diane wasn't a threat. The entire time she was talking, Warren and Rashad were looking at each other as if thinking the same thing: *Women are crazy.* Then Chantal looked at Dream and said, "Wow, you look more like your aunt Charisma than your mama."

Warren tightened his grip on Chantal's hand without realizing it. This gave Chantal the signal that something wasn't right and that she was on to something. Rashad noticed it as well, and they both began to look closer at Dream. I tried to sit up in the bed so that I could get a good look as well. Chantal was standing in my way, but all of a sudden, she moved out of the way so that I could see. She looked back at me with an expression as if to say, "Do you see what I see?" It was our twin intuition. She knew I would want to see what was going on. She began to speak louder. "As a matter of fact, Rashad, she looks like you too."

Diane tapped Dream and told her to go down the hall to the waiting room. As Dream took her first steps, Rashad gently grabbed her arm and asked, "How old are you, Dream?"

She politely answered, "I'm fifteen."

He let her go and looked at Warren and then Diane. The looks on their faces told it all. At that moment, we knew what everyone had been scared we would find out: Dream was Charisma and Rashad's child. Rashad rushed down the hallway with Warren behind him. Chantal left Diane in the hallway and came back into my room. "Kendra, don't worry, because we still have one up."

I looked at her with a confused face.

"I have to talk quickly before Rashad comes back. In a nutshell, Rashad doesn't know that you lost the baby."

"What!" I screamed.

Placing her finger over her lips, she said, "Shhh. Rashad wasn't in here when the doctor came in with the report. I told her that I was the only relative and that if you lost the baby, I would be the one to tell you when you woke up. Don't get all upset when I tell you this, because at the end of the day, you will win."

Sitting up in the bed, I asked, "Win what, Chantal? What is going on?"

She lowered her voice and said, "Win Rashad. Look, Charisma and Rashad were in the ambulance you hit."

"What!" I screamed.

After telling me to shush once more, Chantal continued. "I don't know what is going on between them, but it doesn't matter. You and I both know that Rashad is a good man. If you want to save your marriage, you need to act like you just found out that you are pregnant. Right now, he is probably cursing Charisma out for keeping his child from him."

"His child," I said sadly. The words gave me a heartache.

"Rashad just found out that Dream is his fifteen-year-old child that he never knew about just a few seconds ago. I know it's fucked up, but we don't have to marinate in that, Kendra. He didn't even know, but now that we know, that knowledge is power. You can replace his anger with joy by making him think he can have the chance to see his child grow up from the beginning. You are in the position to win right now, and you don't even know it."

By the look in her eyes, I could tell she was proud of her plan. "So what do I do when it's time for me to start showing, genius?" I said.

She looked at me and smiled. "You better get to work on getting pregnant for real then. Tick tock."

CHAPTER 8

Jullian

Two months had passed since the deaths of Boss and West, Charisma's accident, the revelation that Dream was Rashad and Charisma's, and my realization that Daddy was sick. I didn't tell my sisters the real reason I asked Warren and Chantal to come stay with me. They thought it was because I was still grieving over West, but I really invited them because my daddy was getting sicker, and Chantal needed an extra hand. We had been spending a lot of time together. I got a part-time job with Chantal at the spa just to get out of the house. Of course, I didn't need the money, because West had left me well off. My daddy was physically taken care of but was slipping into depression. He never wanted to watch movies, eat with us, or go out with us. He felt as if he were a burden because we had to walk slower for him. I wished he didn't feel that way. Things could have been worse. He sat in his room or out on his room's balcony all day, listening to music or watching TV. Chantal said, "Well, at least he is doing something."

After a full day of shopping, Chantal cooked dinner while I ironed Daddy's clothes for the entire week. He didn't go out, but he was a man who believed in wearing nice clothes every day just in case. I had been lonely since West died. Taking care of my father gave me something to do. I still had all of West's and my pictures up, and I still cried myself to sleep sometimes.

Shoving the spoon in my face when I returned to the kitchen, Chantal said, "Taste this." I licked my lips after tasting her special sauce for the chicken. It was good. Chantal could really cook.

Having her there made my day better, since the rest of my family had been recovering over the past three months. My father trusted her, so I felt comfortable with her being around. Plus, with her being there, I had help overseeing my father but time to go cry if needed to. I didn't have to stay strong all of the time. It was hard to keep this secret from the rest of the family. This secret bonded Chantal and I in a way we would have never bonded otherwise. I was glad I had confronted Daddy and Mom about what I overheard in the bathroom. Mom didn't want to burden me with more bad news, but she was glad someone else knew besides her. She loved the idea that he was staying with me and not with Chantal. She didn't trust Chantal—but who trusted the next woman anyway? Normally, Mom's instincts were right, but I chalked up her distrust to slight jealousy.

Charisma's world turned upside down as she tried to make it up to Dream that she had not told her that she was her mother. She didn't have time for anything extra. Dad's illness would have been too much for her during this time. Thank God Dream had a good relationship with the Lord. She didn't make it hard on Charisma. Rashad moved back in with Kendra to help her recover. The fact that they were expecting and that Rashad was still mad at Charisma for keeping secrets helped. Secretly, I was rooting for Rashad and Charisma to reunite. There was something about Darnelle that I did not like. I couldn't place my finger on it and didn't have time to. As my mother always said, "It will come out in the wash." I'd just wait because Charisma seemed to be happy, and he wasn't my man. Adrianna was in her own world, making money with Diamond. Since Diamond had fallen out with Sly, her only family member, over Boss's death, Adrianna had taken her home from the hospital and nursed her back to health. Adrianna was all about that money, but I kept telling her that money wasn't everything. I wouldn't trust the bitch. I was a little jealous that they spent so much time together. I didn't know if Adrianna was keeping Diamond close because she had forgiven her and they were friends or if she was keeping her close because she hadn't forgotten and still viewed Diamond as the enemy. I always said, "Once a snake, always a snake." They were bosses now, and bosses didn't have a lot of time for family. Charisma had been able to stop Officer Styles from continuing to investigate Adrianna—something about her having an ace in her back pocket with Judge Ross. Nothing could stop them now but themselves.

"Damn, that was good. I can't gain any weight, Chantal. You are going to make me too fat to fit into my bridesmaid dress." Charisma and Darnelle had moved the wedding date up, and they were getting married next weekend. Darnelle said the accident had made him realize that life was too short and that waiting an entire year to get married was too long to wait. "Call me when dinner is ready, Chantal. I need to go work out first, so when I eat, my metabolism will be built up," I said, leaving the kitchen.

Instead of going down the hallway to the gym, I went to my room to get on my private stripper pole. I put on some Waka Flocka to get crunk. I slipped on my sexy black booty shorts and let my titties hang out. I liked to look at them bounce in the mirror when I was on the pole doing my sexy moves. West used to love it. I hadn't had sex since he died, so pleasing myself was the only way to get that monkey off my back. If someone had just blown on it, man, it would have been a wrap, but no one could get close enough in my space. My days were filled with Chantal and Daddy.

After reaching to the top of the pole, I slid halfway down before I started my routine. I used to sneak out and strip at Nikki's years ago, when I was a teenager, before I went to finish up high school with Ms. Josephine. While working there, I learned a lot of what not to do. I only stopped because Ms. Josephine didn't play. I couldn't sneak out while living with her.

To my surprise, Chantal was watching me in my doorway. "Dinner is ready," she said as she walked away.

After dinner, I grabbed a good book and tried to get my mind off of the same before-bed thoughts about West that came every night before I went to sleep. I hated going to bed sad, lonely, and horny. I drifted off and started dreaming of West climbing in bed behind me and lightly touching my nipples with his hands. Once my nipples became rock hard, he licked down my stomach to my pleasure. He rotated his tongue across my clit and then stuck his tongue in. *Damn,* I thought to myself. This time was better than ever before. It was getting so good that I grabbed his head to push his tongue in harder, because I was about to cum. When I did, I woke up, because his head was full of silky black hair. It wasn't West—it was Chantal! She looked up at me and saw me staring at her in disbelief. She started going in for the kill then. I wanted to ask her what the fuck she was doing, but by that time, I had cum in her mouth.

CHAPTER 9

Adrianna

"If I was gay, you would get it, Adrianna," Diamond said, laughing as I leaned over her to wash her hair.

"If I feel the slightest touch on my nipples, I'm going to drown your ass in this sink, Diamond." We laughed. Neither of us would ever trade in dick for pussy. At least I wouldn't.

For the past three months, all we had done was laugh at each other and with each other. You couldn't have paid me to believe just months ago that she and I would be so close. We were a lot alike. Maybe Boss had seen that as well. Even though I had taken her in to live with me, I still kept pictures of Boss and I around the house. I wanted to remind her that she might have been his chick, but I was his woman. I knew I shouldn't care. It wasn't about him. Fuck him. It was about keeping Diamond in her place. She knew she was a boss bitch, but she failed to realize that there were other boss bitches too. I was one of them.

We ran ship just like Boss and West had. The original crew, a.k.a. the Loyals, wanted to make their money, and to my surprise, most of them had no problem with who was in charge. They just wanted to make their money the same way they'd been making it. Lady had been next in line to take Diamond's place at the safe house when Boss and West ran ship. She was now the lead Loyal. She had been around from the beginning. She was dark skinned, tall, slim, and runway-model pretty. She wasn't hood pretty or video pretty with curves, so I'd never worried about her around Boss. We also didn't have to worry about her looking as if she were carrying weight as she moved in and out of customs or with the police. She got pulled over by the police one time off B-Ford which is one of the most popular streets in Charlotte. They let her go, telling her she didn't look like she was from around there and to get home safely. I laughed just thinking about it. I didn't know her that well. She always did her job and did it on time. She was dependable, and that was why we kept her around. She didn't talk much, but those were the ones you had to watch. Diamond said it wasn't her but her lack of street maturity that she didn't trust. Lady was green to a certain degree on the streets. Although she was dependable and kept her mouth shut, we knew that her greenness on the streets could be deadly to our organization. However, so far, she had passed every task. Diamond and I decided to buy her the latest S-Class Benz to show her our appreciation for her loyalty, keep her loyalty, and show the other Loyals how loyalty was rewarded. They didn't have to start from the bottom again, nor did they have to have their cash flow interrupted. The fact that Diamond and I had slid into Boss's and West's positions meant they didn't have to take the risk of trusting the competition in the game. Diamond informed me that she had continued handling everything after Boss and West were murdered. She knew the Jamaican connection, so our Loyals stayed paid. We called our crew Loyals to remind them that loyalty was everything, and if someone proved that it wasn't, we would make sure that person lost everything, which meant his or her life. Diamond had sunup to sundown, and I had sundown to sunup with check-ins. Her brother Sly wanted a cut, but Diamond said hell no, and my answer was hell no. She said he was too desperate. Desperate niggas ended up as dead niggas, and dead niggas were bad for business. She always said that the head had to be on lock with one common focus: money. When people got their feelings involved, people got hurt. When people got hurt, people got killed. She said Sly had been jealous of Boss and West, which had caused him to act on his emotions. We decided to keep him around in case we needed to use him to do some dirt. You didn't have to pay a desperate nigga much to be dirty. At first, I thought she was just trying to save him because he was her brother. However, she had a point that he'd already proven he had no problem laying niggas down if he had to. Lastly, he owed us for killing Boss and West instead of just robbing them, as Diamond had instructed him to. People had to follow protocol, or bosses wouldn't deal with them. We had no room for live wires. Diamond said he spent most of his time with some new chick who really had him open. She said they'd be on some Bonnie-and-Clyde ish. She hadn't met the girl yet but had promised him that if he stayed with her for more than six months, she would.

Even though I let Diamond into my heart, I would never let her into my mind. The mind could play tricks on you sometimes, and I had to always have a clear head. In case she tried to burn me, I made sure I never touched anything at any of our naked safe houses. I always went through the front door instead of the back, because the cameras only worked in the back. I kept that secret in my back pocket. Boss had set the cameras up like that to keep himself clean. Everyone, including West, would be on camera, except him, because West also went through the back on occasion. The camera feed ran to Boss's and my house. Neither Diamond nor West had ever had a need to look at it. They wouldn't have unless something had popped off. If it had, the excuse that we were just as shocked as they were that the front cameras didn't work would have been good enough as a cover. Boss had never wanted to set West up. He'd just felt you should never trust anyone 100 percent. I had taken a mental note. On the outside, looking in, it had appeared that Boss and I were taking a risk by using the front—and that was how it was supposed to appear. The front cameras were just for show to make it seem as if we had extra security. Anybody in his or her right mind would go to the back if wanting to commit a crime. Since Diamond always went through the back to keep a low profile, she was the only one on camera. I always let her do the inspection and check the safe hidden behind a picture on the office wall. Therefore, her fingerprints were the only ones there. The real money was in the office bathroom's vent, because no one but the cops would think of that. I kept it there for safekeeping, because someone was always at work at the safe house. It would be my emergency money if I ever needed it.

"Have you heard from Sly? And whose turn is it to cook dinner tonight?" I asked, pouring us a glass of wine to drink while waiting for her hair to air dry. She could let her hair air dry, and it would curl up and look pretty naturally. I started laughing when I handed her glass to her, because for the first month, Diamond would not let me cook for her unless she watched me cook the food, and she would only drink bottled drinks. She didn't fully trust me, and I didn't blame her. There were times when I still wanted to kill the hoe.

"Yes, he checked in. He checked in ten minutes late, saying he had no signal at the mall, but he checked in. His new girl has him spending stacks on a regular now. When we slow down, I might have to meet her sooner than I thought," she said, pouring herself a second glass of wine.

"Love will have you fucked up. That's why I don't entertain it," I said as I clinked her wine glass with mine. "Cheers!"

Now that time had passed, we both felt as if we had been missing out on each other for all of these years. Though she was now fully recovered, neither one of us had mentioned her moving out. There was no reason to. The mansion was big. The only thing we didn't have enough room for was all of the different cars and trucks she had. She liked to trade out to stay under the radar. She had a warehouse full of new and old cars, stashed in case she had to make a run for it. Therefore, having her there wasn't a problem. We loved each other's company. We'd even decided to get a baby-blue-eyed pit bull next week. We'd already decided to name him Boss in order to honor Boss for his doggish ways. We laughed every time we thought about it. We were friends whether we liked it or not. I couldn't ex her out if I wanted to now, because she'd peeped on Darnelle as he was leaving one night, when she'd had nothing but time on her hands to be nosy during her recovery.

He was like Diamond with a penis and a different smell. Sometimes I felt like Diamond's wife but Darnelle's girlfriend. I felt like Diamond's wife because I had done everything for her and been everything to her while she was down. I felt like Darnelle's girlfriend because it wasn't always about sex with him. We actually used to cuddle up to watch our favorite shows and have Netflix nights. I liked street boys, but I liked the time Darnelle provided. Street boys didn't always have the time that I needed. Darnelle was a hustler too but in a different way. He knew how to manipulate people to do what he wanted. That power turned me on. I learned a lot from him as I overheard his business calls. He was a lawyer—and a high-profile lawyer at that. I absorbed everything when in his presence.

Before Diamond got back on her feet, I was at home plenty of nights, which left the door open for Darnelle to come over more at night. I loved being with him, and he loved being with me. He just didn't love me—yet.

"I'm going to run a warm bath after the show goes off, and I want you to join me," Darnelle said in a matter-of-fact tone during one of the commercial breaks of *Scandal*. I felt guilty watching this with him, knowing that *Scandal* was Diamond's and my show. I knew she was upstairs, watching it all alone. We missed each other's company so much during the show that we kept texting each other during the commercial breaks. Darnelle sensed that we were not happy watching it separately, so he volunteered to go get Diamond and bring her downstairs to the master bedroom with us.

When we opened the door to help her down the stairs, she was lying across the bed with a simple but sexy black silk Victoria's Secret gown on. I admired a bitch that kept it sexy even if just for herself. I saw Darnelle looking seductively at her, but I couldn't blame him. I got the same rise he did when we opened the door. I wasn't sure if I felt that way because she was sexy or because of the look in his eyes, which openly admitted that he was turned on by her sexiness. Either way, I couldn't get mad. Darnelle wasn't my man, and any man would have looked at Diamond the same way. Instead of us carrying her down to our room, she signaled for us to get in the bed with her, because the show had come back on. Huck and Papa Pope were about to meet, and we didn't want to miss the scene. So we got under the covers with her. Darnelle hesitated at first, but when he saw me pat the area beside me, he got in. Diamond was to my left, and Darnelle was to my right. I was in the middle. We sat there, lost in thought, watching *Scandal* and eating the rest of the kettle popcorn that Diamond had. We forgot how awkward the moment was, because

Kerry Washington and Huck were giving us life through the show.

When it was over, Diamond said she was going to run a bath in the Jacuzzi and relax with some wine. She still needed help going up and down the stairs and carrying heavy things, but she could manage the little things. We had a maid clean the house, so cleaning was never a concern for her. Darnelle and I were trying to clean all of the kettle corn out of Diamond's bed, when we heard her come back into the room, clearing her throat. We both turned around to look at her. When she got our attention, she dropped her black slip sexily to the floor and asked seductively, "Are you going to join me?"

Darnelle and I looked at each other as if to say, "Why not?" The water was the perfect temperature. The smell of cherry vanilla was in the air from the candles Diamond had lit. The bubbles were sky high and soothing to my skin. While we were in the Jacuzzi, naked, Diamond thanked us for joining her. "Let me be clear: this is not a threesome," she said with a laugh. "I've been down for so long recovering that I forgot what sex smells like. Now I have a chance to watch it live," she said with a grin.

Before I could wrap my head around what she was suggesting, Darnelle cupped both of my breasts with his hands, sucking on both of my nipples at the same time. The thought of her watching turned him on. The thought of him being turned on again turned me on. Diamond slid behind him in the water so that her face was facing mine. She placed his back on her breasts. The feeling of breasts on his back and breasts in his mouth got him harder than I'd ever seen. She then reached out to me and placed me on his manhood. She stared at me with a look of seduction, directly in my eyes, as I rode him into pure ecstasy. I would close my eyes, and when I opened them, she was still looking at me, enjoying every moment in her view. She then lifted her left leg up and began to please herself as she watched us. She grabbed my hair with her right hand over

Darnelle's right shoulder and massaged her clit with her left hand until she came. Seeing her close her eyes as she came made me cum all over Darnelle. Afterward, she got up and jumped into the separate shower, thanking us as she turned the water on. That was our signal to leave. I felt used and cheap, but I had fun. Darnelle and I showered together, and then he left to go home. I didn't know where he told my sister Charisma he was during these long nights, but I didn't care. We never spoke of that night again.

For the longest time, Diamond would call me to help her down the stairs. The master bedroom was on the first floor. I never thought she would come down by herself so soon. I was wrong. She was doing much better. She was even going out of the house without me sometimes. It felt good having someone to talk to about Darnelle and me. I was falling, and she always picked on me for doing so. She said I was dick-whipped. I never admitted it to her, but I was. "I haven't seen Darnelle the past few weeks. Did you put him on pussy punishment, Adrianna?" Diamond said, pouring herself a second glass of wine.

"Try dick punishment. The closer he and Charisma get to their wedding date, the more distant he becomes. As of now, he won't even return any of my calls or texts. I guess he is done. It had to end one day. I just thought it would at least last until the night of their wedding. Even if he wanted to continue, I can't mess with a married man."

Diamond turned the TiVo on. We wanted to finish watching the *Scandal* episode from last night. We had gone on a double date last night with Terrell Jackson and Marco Falls from the Carolina Panthers. We had the best time last night at Del Frisco's in South Park. Shaking her head at me, Diamond said, "Girl, your morals are messed up. They are all gray. You can sleep with your sister's fiancé, but you won't sleep with a married man. Child, boo! I'm either black or white. It saves you a lot of regret and heartache. I either give a fuck or less than a fuck."

I plopped down on the couch beside her and said, "I know, I know. He got me messed up in the head right now, but I will be all right in due time. I always am." I could tell she didn't believe me. We went ahead and watched *Scandal* to get caught up. We knew we had limited time, because we had to do a surprise visit at the naked safe house that night. We had to make sure they remembered who was boss.

CHAPTER 10

Jullian

I kept telling myself each time that this time would be the last time I slept with Chantal. I couldn't believe she turned me out. A woman really knew another woman's body. She licked and sucked everywhere possible. I loved the feeling, but I hated that it was from a woman. I had to get away from her, but the fact that she and Daddy lived there was messing things up. Most of the time, we would go out to her candy-apple-red Corvette and make love. We would go to the airpark at the airport and watch the planes take off. On most nights, we would be the only car there. I would lie down on the hood and let her eat me out. The sound of the planes combined with the sound of her moaning was explosive for me. I loved being around her, and I tried to keep our relationship platonic, but at least three times a week, she gave me a sexy look, and my body became weak. Any woman would have been attracted to her full lips, nice hips, seductive eyes, and half-Korean and half-black features.

I tried to get Daddy to be around us more, but he wouldn't budge from his depression. Ms. Josephine had been coming over more, because she was the only one who could get him to go to his doctor appointments and smile. He would do anything for that woman. Chantal made it seem as if Josephine were the only person who could get him to go, so I thought, *So be it.* If Daddy would have let us tell Charisma and Adrianna that he was sick, that would have given me somebody else to talk to about his situation. Chantal was my only outlet now.

Ms. Josephine and Daddy left that morning to go to breakfast before his appointment. Neither Chantal nor Dr. Joseph knew that Mama and Daddy went out to eat before or after appointments. When Chantal was at work, Mama and Daddy would cuddle up on his bedroom balcony, listening to old-school jams and laughing for hours. Otis Redding, Luther Vandross, and Atlantic Starr were just a few of the musical artists they played. They were getting closer, and he and Chantal couldn't have been further apart. She didn't even sleep in the bed with him anymore. She slept in one of the guest rooms most nights. The other nights, she snuck downstairs to my bedroom. I knew Mr. Joseph couldn't be happy about Mama spending all this time with Daddy. I wondered if he even knew.

On my way back to the house from my morning run, I saw Mr. Joseph's black Bentley come flying past me, leaving from the direction of my house. I was only three houses away, but considering these houses were mansions, I was still five minutes away from the house. I knew Mama and Daddy were at the house. Daddy's appointment wasn't until ten o'clock, and it was eight o'clock. That meant Mama and Daddy were getting their grown-up time in early. I reached for my cell to call one of them to warn them but quickly realized I didn't have it on me.

I arrived at the house and immediately jumped in the shower then climbed into bed. Mama and Daddy were still in his room. Chantal was already at work. She faithfully went in at seven every morning. To my surprise, a few minutes later, I heard Chantal come back to the house. She said, "They think I don't know, but I know. I really don't even care what they do. I just care that they think that I'm stupid enough not to notice."

I just lay there with the cover over my face.

"I know they're your parents, so I'm not expecting you to say anything. I just wanted you to know that I know. Mr. Joseph called me and—"

Before she could finish, I interrupted and asked, "Mr. Joseph? Mama's Mr. Joseph?"

"Oh wow, shit just got real," she said, sitting on the edge of my bed. She smelled good. I prayed she would not touch me. To my surprise, she didn't. She got up and said, "Breakfast will be ready in about ten minutes, so get up."

I took the other hallway to my father's room. "Daddy?" I whispered as I lightly knocked on the door.

"Yes, baby girl?" He answered as if he were in the middle of something.

"Daddy, Chantal is in the kitchen, cooking. She came back early," I said firmly, still trying to whisper. I heard the bed make a noise and the sound of feet moving. Now I knew for sure what Daddy was in the middle of—my mama! I could tell they were putting their clothes back on, because I heard both of them get out of the bed and fumble around the room. I left out the part about Mr. Joseph. I figured I would tell Mom later. I didn't want to stress out Daddy with that information, but I couldn't let them walk out and be surprised to see Chantal back home.

Mama opened the door and brushed by me to leave, giving me a smile that said, "Well, now she knows." Daddy was a few steps behind her, looking like a kid caught in the cookie jar. Mama's phone vibrated. Then, all of a sudden, Mama stopped walking. She turned to Daddy to show him the text. I looked over Daddy's shoulder to be nosy. I wanted to read it too because I could tell by her reaction that it was from Mr. Joseph. The text read, "Ask Warren—how did my dick taste in his mouth?"

"Come on, Warren—we have to get to your doctor," Mama said, trying to get Daddy out of the house so that they could discuss matters without me being nosy. I just laughed and then waited to see if Chantal was going to say something as they left.

As they were leaving, Chantal was standing by the front door with two coffee mugs in her hands. One was for Daddy, and the other one was for Mama. Extending them, she said, "Good morning, you two. Hot coffee, just the way you like it."

My father paused. My mother took the mug meant for her and sarcastically said with a smile, "Don't be rude, Warren. Take the coffee. It's hot—just the way you like it, baby." Chantal let out a slight grin and opened the front door for them. My father took the coffee while he and Mama walked out. Chantal just stood there for a few seconds, watching them go down the front steps, and then turned around to head to the kitchen, leaving the front door wide open. As I went to close the door, laughing at my mom's diva attitude toward Chantal, I saw Mama pour her and Daddy's coffee out directly onto Chantal's red Corvette. I laughed inside.

When I smelled the bacon and fresh coffee, I got up, slipped on my pink Carolina Panthers jersey, and went to the kitchen. Chantal had put a dish of freshly chopped strawberries and pineapples on the counter with a pitcher of orange juice. "When the bagels are ready, breakfast will be served," she said, moving in between my legs as I sat on the counter. She slid her hands up my brown thighs and whispered, "I love you, Jullian," in my ear. I felt goose bumps. Then she poured a little bit of orange juice over my breasts and began to suck on them. She leaned me back with her right hand and grabbed fruit with her left. She squeezed strawberry and pineapple juice onto my cookie and began to eat it for breakfast.

I was in ecstasy, when I heard Daddy say, "Make sure you don't use all of the fruit. I might get hungry later, and I need to eat healthy." I jumped up and looked in the direction of his voice, but he'd already walked up the stairs.

CHAPTER 11

Adrianna

Diamond and I had the best time at the Dolce and Gabbana showcase fashion show in New York. We spent fifty stacks in a matter of three days. We had dates lined up with models and music executives every day we were there. I loved that girl, and I knew she loved me. We'd become best friends, and I wouldn't have traded her in for anyone. We played, but we laid with no one the entire weekend. We shared a suite and made sure that every date was a double date. We went out together, and we left together. That way, those niggas knew they were not getting any this time around. We were putting them through the girlfriend-approval test, little did they know. Diamond had to approve mine, and I had to approve hers. If one passed the test, then we would fly back up for a second date, or he would fly back down for a second date. Sometimes your bestie could see what you couldn't see. Diamond and I were a lot alike, so we trusted each other's judgment.

On the way home, in the airport, we saw Nelly with his fine self. He and his crew were checking us out. They gave us the signal to come over, but we didn't date rappers. They got photographed too much, and the life Diamond and I were in meant no pictures. It was the downside of being a boss, but on that note, we had to pass. Nelly could have gotten it in another lifetime but not this lifetime. When we got back to the Queen City, we did a pop-up at the safe house. Everything seemed to be in order. It was eight o'clock in the morning. I had jet lag, and all I wanted to do was sleep.

Diamond cooked us breakfast and then took our dog, Boss, out running with her.

"DivaStar won't see me today," I said to myself when I hit the snooze button. I heard my bedroom door open. I waited for Diamond to do something stupid to wake me up, such as slapping me on my ass, as she normally did. Instead, I felt a cloth and hand over my mouth.

When I woke up, I was in a barn with no lights. My hands and legs were tied to a wooden pole in the middle of the barn, and I had tape over my mouth. I was barefoot. The air was so thick and hot that I could barely breathe. It seemed no one had been in there for a while to let air in and out. My legs were sore, and my head was spinning. I was going to fuck up whoever had me in this filthy place. I kept telling myself to man up and cry later. Clearly, this was a do-or-die situation, and tears wouldn't help me. I swallowed the lump in my throat and decided to make a plan of escape. I started to move up and down on the wooden pole so that it could scratch against the ropes. *Fucking amateurs!* I thought. *They should have just killed me, because when I find out who they are, I'm sure as hell going to kill them.* I felt the rope on my hands getting looser, and then it broke. I pulled my small switchblade from out of my silky black ponytail and was ready to slice and dice the first person I saw on sight.

It was dark, but a little bit of moonlight was shining through the cracks of the wood. I walked slowly, trying not to fall over anything—or anyone, for that matter. I kept running into spider webs, so I was beyond pissed. I came to what I thought might be an exit. I ran my fingers over the large wooden door, trying to locate the handle, because I could barely see anything. My hand caught on a splinter. *Dammit!* I yelled in my head. I didn't want to make a sound in case someone could hear me. I found the latch and was out of there so fast that I didn't even realize when I started running. The next thing I knew, I was running across some grass to a dirt road lit up by the moonlight. I looked up at the stars and knew I was running north. Rocks were cutting my feet, but I was running too fast to notice the pain. I was sure I would feel it later. I imagined running like a track star back in high school in order to keep myself from being scared. I still had the blade in my hand. I didn't have a second to waste, so I just ran and ran until I saw headlights. My first thought was *Don't go all the way out into the road, in case it is the person who put you in the barn.* Then I thought, *Adrianna, that shit only happens in the movies.* So I waved down the truck that was heading in my direction. It was a newly released black Escalade. At least it wasn't a beat-up truck with crazies in it like the one in the movie *Wrong Turn.* This might not have been West Virginia, but any city outside of Charlotte in North Carolina was suspect to me. The truck stopped suddenly right in front of me, so fast that the motorcycle it was carrying slid off the back of the truck. The driver's-side door opened. I saw a man's fresh pair of Louies, and then I saw the man's face. It was Sly.

My eyes got big. His eyes were full of anger. I shot off running into the woods, but as soon as I reached the woods, I tripped over a log. "Get up, bitch!" Sly said, standing over me.

I didn't say a word. I was mad and hurt at the same time—mad at this motherfucker for having me in the backwoods somewhere and hurt because Diamond had set my ass up. I made my mind up at that point that I was going to kill him the first chance I got. As for her, I had other plans. My plan for her required her to live in misery every day while seeing me stack my money and mourning the loss of her brother and her plush life. I felt that punishment was better than death. "You know what your problem is, Adrianna? You think you know everything," he said, looking down at me, waiting for me to ask him for help to get up. "I kept telling Diamond at the hospital that I didn't kill Boss, but she wouldn't believe me."

Debating if I should kick him in the balls or not, I asked with an attitude, "Who killed him then?"

"The fuck if I know. Diamond might have done it. Shit! It wouldn't be the first nigga she put in a body bag," he said, laughing.

I thought, *What if he is right?* Then I remembered Diamond's confession at the graveside, and I knew she wasn't the one who'd killed Boss and West.

"What I look like robbing a nigga myself? Boss wasn't even there when my people raided the naked safe house. That was planned on purpose. I sent my goons in to do that with strict orders not to kill anybody unless they had to, and they didn't have to. My girl—your Loyal Lady at the naked safe house—conveniently didn't set the alarm after she entered for work that day, so we could just slip in." My eyes showed my disappointment that Lady had betrayed us. "Diamond called out so that she wouldn't be blamed for the robbery. She knew we were going to hit the naked safe house that day. My people slipped in when she had all the girls in the review meeting they have every morning to get their instructions and pat down for the day. You know, Lady patted them girls down when they entered and when they left to make sure them hoes didn't steal anything. I waited outside in the cut to make sure it went as I ordered, and it did. When my men pulled off, I saw a black Suburban go around to the back, and a minute later, I saw Boss pull up to the front. I found out later you were in the car with Boss, and minutes later, he was killed. I told Diamond this over and over, but she refused to hear it. I think she believed me, but she wanted to use that as an excuse not to cut me in with you two after Boss and West's murder. So fuck her!"

I could tell he was telling the truth. I couldn't help but think, *If he didn't kill Boss and West, then who did?* "I need help getting up. I think I twisted my ankle," I told him. I was lying because I wanted him to think I was weaker than I was so that he wouldn't be on guard. "Hold on to me." He picked me up to help me walk to the car, knowing he still had to kill me because I would eventually kill him. I saw a thick stick and said,

"Hold up. Let me use this as a cane. That way, I don't have to put all my weight on you."

He started laughing and said, "I'm not worrying about that. I can handle all of that and then some, but go ahead, because I don't want my clothes dirty anyway."

I rolled my eyes at him, because who kidnapped someone while wearing the latest Louie Vuitton from head to toe anyway? *Niggas!* When we got to the truck, he tried to help me in like a gentleman. I looked at him as if he'd lost his damn mind. He had a laptop and duffle bag in the front seat. "Can you move the stuff out of the front seat first?" I asked. When he leaned over to move the items out of the front seat, I picked up the thick stick I was using as a cane and stuck him right in the booty hole. I would have hit him first, but I was scared the stick would break, so I went for the booty hole. "Fuck you, bastard!" I screamed as I tossed him down to the ground.

Holding his bottom, he screamed, "You bitch! I'm going to get you!"

The truck was still running, so I jumped into the driver's seat and pulled off. I stopped at the first gas station. No one was there except for the attendant, an elderly white man. I ran in and said, "Please call 911." He immediately picked the phone up. Then I thought, *What the hell am I thinking? Revenge is a must.* I grabbed the phone out of his hand and called Darnelle. After the third ring, he answered.

"Hello?"

"Darnelle, it's me—Adrianna. Sly and Diamond kidnapped me! Please help!" I quickly said.

"What?" Darnelle said in shock.

"Diamond set me up! Open the envelope I left you the day of Charisma's car accident. You will know what to do with it when you open it. After the wedding tomorrow, I'm going to go into hiding for the next few days, but—" Then I heard shots fired. The elderly attendant took two shots to the chest. He didn't move or make another sound once he hit the floor. It scared me so bad that I dropped the phone.

"You know you fucked up, right?" Sly said behind me with a gun pointed at the back of my head. He dragged me out of the store and forced me into the truck. On the way out, I saw a black Mustang on black wheels with black tint that hadn't been there before. I hoped they were calling the police. He forcefully, by my hair, made me get back in the truck. We drove back toward the barn. It was as if I were in a bad dream. I was in a nightmare, and he was Freddy Krueger. As soon as we pulled down the dirt road that led to the barn, he stopped the truck. He reclined his seat, unzipped his pants, grabbed my head, and forced it toward his dick. This nightmare couldn't have been any worse, I thought. I knew then that the only way I could possibly make it out of there alive was to give him the best blow job ever. Maybe he would keep me alive a little bit longer to have a second run with me. That would buy me more time to escape. I sucked and licked him as if he were Boss. I even moaned and called him Daddy. He couldn't believe how into it I was, considering he had a nine to my head. When I beat his dick against my tongue while staring him straight in his eyes, he almost had a heart attack. With one more suck, he was done. He came in my mouth. I was about to open the door to spit it out, when he pushed the gun deeper into my temple and said, "Swallow it." So I did. Then he said with a smirk, "Get on this dick, and if you ride it well enough, I might let you live another day." I didn't move. "Oh, so you want me to take it, huh? That's even better. I like it rough," he said, flipping me over and then positioning himself on top of me.

Right before he put it in, I heard *pow, pow, pow*. Sly fell on top of me. The driver's-side door opened as I pushed Sly off of me. "Adrianna, are you okay?" I heard a familiar voice say. It was Diamond. She was the one in the black Mustang. She immediately hugged me and then looked at her brother. He looked straight at her with blood coming out of his mouth, trying to breathe.

She scorned him by saying, "You know you fucked up again, right?" Then she shot him again—this time in the head.

That night, Diamond called everyone to the safe house. We knew the crowd included the guilty and the innocent. It was time for us to make a clear statement that would forever go down in the history of the game. Diamond told Siri to call Lady. When Lady answered, she tried her best to sound sleepy, but we knew that bitch was up, waiting for Sly to confirm the hit. Little did she know, she was the target that night.

"Hi, Dia. What's good, boss?" she said in her fake sleepy voice. I was so mad at hearing her voice that I was calm. With Diamond by my side, all I could think of was revenge. It was the only cool glass of water that could put out the fire that was blazing in my heart for betrayal. Loyalty was everything, because without it, you had nothing.

"I haven't heard from Adrianna, which tells me something is off. Meet me at the safe house so that we can put our heads together on our next move."

"When? Because I just started putting a perm on my head. It has to sit for a few minutes before I wash it out. I can just let it air dry or just B-boy style it with a fitted hat. I promise I will come directly after that."

Diamond said with a commanding and fake polite voice, "Lady?"

"Yes?"

"If I don't hear from Adrianna in the next twenty-four hours, be prepared to be up next." Silence filled the air as we waited for Lady to respond. I could tell Diamond had come up with that bait while on the phone with the traitor. I had to admit that Diamond was a boss for that. She began to drive the Mustang faster down the highway. I could tell she was just as eager as I was to put one through the head of the enemy who'd betrayed us. Every second she stayed on the phone, she drove faster down Highway 74.

We knew Lady had been waiting on this opportunity ever since she and Sly had plotted against me. She knew that Diamond would promote her in the event of my death. Not only would she get promoted, but also, her boyfriend, Sly, would get in on our operation, which he desperately wanted. She'd plotted a win-win situation, not knowing it was going to be a lose-lose situation by the end of the night. Now, sounding fully awake and confident, Lady replied, "Anything for the Loyals."

"That's all I needed to hear, Lady. See you in an hour. Oh, and, Lady? Drive the S-Class." Then Diamond hung up.

"Thanks, Dia," I said, smirking, not looking her direction. I was too busy looking out my window at the small city lights on the way back to Charlotte. We were on the part of Highway 74 that was two lanes only, as we went through the city of Monroe. The speed limit was thirty-five miles per hour as we traveled through. At a stoplight, I saw a black homeless woman pushing her cart beside the highway. I rolled the window down and handed her a Benjamin. I didn't even look long enough for her reaction before rolling the window back up, because I didn't need anything to take me out of killer mode. I had to ask myself, *Who in the hell lives anywhere in North Carolina outside of the beaches, college towns, or Charlotte?*

Instead of staying straight on the highway, Diamond took the 485 exit toward Lady's house. I didn't ask, because it didn't even matter. As long as Lady was served tonight, I was good. We pulled into the newly developed community slowly. Some of the houses had not even been built yet. I could tell this was a four-bedroom-and-up housing development. It wasn't on my level but was nice. Diamond parked at the end of a dead-end street with no lights and no houses. We could see the back of Lady's house on the hill. All I could see was red. I could barely feel the pain from fighting off Sly and escaping, because revenge was my cure for the night. Reaching in the back for her bag, Diamond said, "Here. We need to put these black clothes on so we can be all blacked out. You are too bright colored and too cute for this mission. Grab the nines too."

I knew the nines were loaded, so I was careful in how I grabbed them. I grabbed the black hoodie and black sweats she handed me and put them over my skinny jeans and fitted T-shirt. "What about shoes? I didn't have any on when your brother took me."

Popping the trunk, she said, "I got you."

We climbed the hill, wearing our all-black outfits. Our faces were half covered with black scarves. The only things not covered in black were our eyes. We were ready for our mission. Diamond kicked the first side door leading into the garage, and I kicked the garage door leading into the house. Just like a Loyal, Lady was on the other side of the door with her gun pointing right at us. Clearly, she'd heard the first door get kicked in. Surprised to see us, she froze for about two seconds. During that time, I already had my pistol to her head. That mistake was detrimental to her life. I was kind of disappointed because we'd taught her better than that. It was not your enemies you had to be ready for but your friends. Diamond grabbed a chair and told her to sit her ass down. She still had perm on her head. Diamond looked at me, and then she looked at Lady, smirking. Now I knew why we had come to her house instead of having her meet us at the safe house with the rest of the Loyals.

They all waited in anticipation of what was yet to come. Everyone was standing in a half circle in the middle of the safe house, waiting for the front door to open. Diamond walked into the middle of the room, holding a garbage bag. I pulled my gun and swept in left to right, daring anyone to say something or pull a gun. Diamond said, "Loyalty is everything. No organization can operate without it. Disloyalty will not be tolerated. We have no problem with anyone disassociating themselves from us if you feel like your time is up. You can't be about the dope game all your life. However, what you won't do is betray us." Diamond shook the bag, and Lady's head fell out and rolled across the floor. Burn marks from her perm told the story of the painful torture we'd made her suffer before she took her last breath. The pain had been so unbearable that she'd kept passing out. I'd raised my gun to put a bullet through her head, but Diamond had had another plan. When our cleanup group had come, she'd asked them to give us the head, because heads were getting ready to roll. Dead silence engulfed the room. It was as if none of the Loyals were even breathing. Neither Diamond nor I showed any remorse in our stance or in our eyes. We didn't want to kill anyone, but we had to do it. That was just the way it was sometimes. It was business but was definitely personal. Our message was sent loud and clear: loyalty was everything.

CHAPTER 12

Kendra

"Come in, Sis!" I yelled to Chantal from my bedroom, which I hadn't left all morning. By now, the sheets were tired of my tears. I hadn't been able to live with the lie any longer, so I'd told Rashad about the baby. Instead of being mad, he was happy as hell. I'd also told him that our divorce was finalized last week. Since he'd already signed the divorce papers, I had signed them and then mailed them in weeks ago.

After we got back together, he was the perfect gentleman, but every day, I checked his sock drawer, and the divorce papers were still there.

He saw them every day when he grabbed a pair of socks, and apparently, it didn't cross his mind to rip them up. I knew then that it was over, so I decided to do him a favor. It was Charisma and Darnelle's wedding day, so I sent Rashad off to stop the wedding.

"You look horrible!" Chantal said, shaking her head at me as she entered the bedroom.

"I know. I will get it together soon but not today," I said, embarrassed.

"Then when, Kendra? You told him that he could go, and he did. That was the test, and he proved you right. Now you know where his heart really is. Pick up your face, and move on, Sis. It's not like Rashad played you or lied to you. Your marriage could have ended worse. Maybe one day you and he could be friends, but for the next few days, it's about you. I need to get you out of this house for a day of shopping. Plus, I need you to be strong for me," she said, throwing the covers back as if to say, "Get up."

"What's wrong, Sis?" I asked.

"I will tell you on the way to the mall. Let's get you showered and get your hair combed first." She stated pushing me into the bathroom.

On the way to the mall, Chantal told me all about the drama she had going on in her life. After Warren had caught her cheating with Jullian, he'd moved out the next day to Ms. Josephine's. Mr. Joseph and Josephine had parted ways. It seemed Warren and Josephine were back together. Only time would tell. The Banks women obviously had a certain effect when it came to winning their men back.

"So if Warren left, why are you so melancholy?" I asked Chantal.

"Jullian made me leave as well. She felt so guilty for letting her father down. She broke my heart, and I can't put it back together, Sis. I don't even know where to start. She wasn't the first woman I've been with, but she was the first woman I ever fell in love with. Actually, she was first person I ever fell in love with," she said, shedding a tear as she turned into the Macy's parking lot at Northlake Mall.

"Oh, wow! I didn't know it ran that deep. It hasn't even been six months yet. I'm surprised you gave your heart to anyone, especially after the childhood we had," I said, trying to forget the bad memories of our childhood.

"I know, Kendra, but women bond faster than men. I don't want to live without her, Sis. I have to find a way to make her understand how much she means to me."

I saw that my sister was heartbroken to no end. I reminded her that Jullian had just lost West and might need some time. She was still dealing with that on top of her father not talking to her because of her relationship with Chantal.

We did some shopping and got our nails done. We walked past a Zales jewelry store, and Chantal wanted to go in. "This ring looks just like the one Jim Jones gave Chrissy in *Love and Hip Hop*. I want this one," she said, tapping the glass. I was in shock. Chantal looked down at her phone and noticed that the wedding was about to start in an hour. "We have to go, Kendra," she said.

"Go where?" I said, looking at her with a strange look.

"We have to go to Charisma's wedding. I have to see Jullian, and I'm going all out this time!"

Even though my husband was going to be there to confess his love to the love of his life, I had no choice but to be ride or die for my sister. At the end of the day, she would always be my sister.

When we pulled up, I saw Rashad pacing back and forth outside the church doors. Everyone else was clearly inside. Rashad was shocked to see me and said, "Kendra, I can't believe you! You sent me here, and now you are trying to stop me?"

I grabbed his hand and said, "No, honey—I mean Rashad. It's not what you think." Chantal jumped out of the car and ran past me into the church as if she didn't have heels on. Holding his hand, I noticed he had already taken his wedding band off, again.

"Oh. Then what's up?" he asked.

I sat down on the top step, drained from all of the drama, and said, "Don't worry about me. I'm not even going inside. Why are you not inside yet? It's about to start."

Taking a seat next to me and placing his hand on his head, he said, "I've been sitting outside the church all morning, waiting for Charisma to arrive so we can talk. However, when she and Dream pulled up, I got the surprise of my life."

"What was that?" I quickly asked, but I immediately regretted asking. I was still in love with my husband, but at the end of the day, he was also still my best friend. I couldn't help it, and best friends always wanted the other person to be happy.

"She looked pregnant, Kendra. I didn't want to believe it, but just like you, she always had a flat stomach. She had a little bump. Plus, what woman gains weight knowing that she is about to get married?" He stood up and started pacing again behind me as I continued to sit on the top step.

"I had to know the truth. So I called Mr. Warren and straight out asked him. He confirmed. Now I don't know what to do. When I went to scream at her in the hospital for not telling me about Dream, she just laid there and took it. I should have known something was wrong then, because even if she is wrong, Charisma is not going to let you talk to her any type of way. The Banks girls are just not built like that. After I finished fussing, she said that she understood if I never wanted to speak to her again and just wanted Dream and I to build a relationship. I just walked out. She didn't try to stop me either. She knew. She knew that she was pregnant, and that's why she let me go. I thought she was only marrying him because I walked away, but the real reason was she already let me go when she found out that she was pregnant at the hospital. I just didn't know about it. Prideful, huh?" He sat back down beside me. "I never wanted to be a baby daddy or a stepdaddy. I only wanted my children by my wife."

I stood up and said, "Yes, but the only wife you ever wanted was Charisma." Silence fell. Then I said on my way back down the white steps of the church, "It took Chantal losing Jullian to realize how much she really loved her. Don't you do the same."

Rashad quickly stood up and said, "What? Huh? Chantal and Jullian!"

I turned around and said, shaking my head, "That's a whole different story, but the point is, life is too short to come up short."

Rashad blew me a kiss to say thank you. He turned around and entered the church. I sat in the car with the windows down, listening to the radio and waiting for Chantal to come back out. Just as I drifted off to sleep, I heard two gun shots. I jumped up and ran toward the church. I had to get my sister out of there. When I got to the church door, I heard two more gun shots.

CHAPTER 13

Adrianna

"Uhm, baby, yes, take all this dick in your mouth."

"I'm sorry, Daddy, for being a naughty girl," I said seductively while preparing to give my man the best lollipop job of his life. I loved it when he talked dirty to me while I was pleasing him. It seemed he'd finally figured out that I was the one for him. After weeks of us arguing and him denying me of this good dick, I was going to suck and swallow every ounce of cum out of him. I wanted to feel him inside of me so bad, but the occasion wouldn't allow it. I was already dripping down my leg from the excitement of tasting him. If I let him put it in, I knew for a fact that cum and wetness would be all over my dress and my Beyoncé ass. I wouldn't have time to clean up before the wedding music started, but it didn't matter, because that night, he would be all mine. I couldn't wait.

Suddenly, I heard footsteps stop right outside the closed door, breaking my concentration. He must have sensed I was about to stop performing, and to my surprise, he grabbed me harder by the head and started groaning. A part of me wanted to stop. I was scared someone would walk in; however, my pussy started thumping with excitement as I realized he was turned on more by the idea that someone was at the door. "I'm about to cum. I'm about to cum! I'm about to cum!!!" he said, his voice growing louder each time he said it. Going faster and deeper, he filled my mouth with warm cum. I smiled on the inside and swallowed. Then I seductively started licking his head to make sure I got all of the cum. I heard the door open just as I was cum'n, but since it didn't seem to faze him, I hadn't even stopped to look. As he was filling my mouth with what could have been our kids, I looked up at him and into his eyes. His eyes were mesmerizing. As he looked in the direction of the dark oak door the church had just replaced, he had a satisfied look in his eyes and a smile on his face.

The next thing I knew, I felt something cold and hard on the side of my head. "Cocked and loaded," I heard a firm voice say. "You might as well stay down, bitch, because you're not getting back up."

Putting his dick back into his pants and scared out of his mind, Darnelle said, "I thought we had a deal. What the fuck are you doing, Diamond?"

Taking the gun off of me and pointing it at him now, Diamond said, "Nigga, since when do I make deals with the devil?"

Still on my knees, I asked, "What deal? What the hell is going on?"

Diamond waved the gun and ordered me to stand up. I was standing there beside Darnelle, confused, pissed, and hurt all at the same time. Diamond was my friend, and Darnelle was supposed to be my man after today. Darnelle had called me to come up to his room. He'd said he should be marrying me, because Charisma wasn't about shit. He'd said he found out that Charisma had cheated on him with Rashad the night before his bachelor party. Mr. Joseph had gotten so drunk that he'd come to the bachelor party to start a fight with my daddy. He was still hurt about Mama taking Daddy back. Mr. Joseph had gotten so mad that he'd told all of the family's secrets, including Charisma cheating with Rashad. Mama must have told him that Dream was Charisma and Rashad's child too. Now Darnelle knew he wouldn't be Charisma's first. I hadn't even known about Charisma's affair until Darnelle had told me last night. I hadn't believed it at first, so I'd called Jullian to confirm it. Jullian hated to lie, but she would never tell. So when I'd straight out asked her, "Did Charisma let Rashad hit it?" she'd told me to call Charisma. That had been all of the confirmation I needed, and it had been for Darnelle as well.

"Diamond, what are you doing?" I yelled. She had just killed her brother last night for me, and now I was at the other end of her gun. I was confused.

"Ask your so-called man why I'm here, Adrianna, and, nigga, you better tell the truth, for every lie is a bullet in your direction," she said, holding the gun like a gangster and pointing it at Darnelle, probably just as she had held it the night she'd killed Sly.

She was serious too. I knew she would shoot, because I'd seen her do it before. I was shocked because this time, she would have witnesses. She must have read my mind. That was the downside of letting a hoe get too close to you.

"You really think I didn't think this out? No one saw me come in, and no one will see me leave. This will clearly look like a love triangle that went wrong when I get done. Between the text messages in your phone and the cum stains on your dress, it shouldn't be hard for the police to figure this situation out." My heart was beating a mile a minute, and I could tell Darnelle's was too. Tapping him on the head with the tip of the gun, she told Darnelle to tell me what was going on. He was standing straight ahead, facing Diamond, but his eyes were looking back and forth between Diamond and I.

"When you called me, Adrianna, from the gas station, I did what you told me to do. I opened the envelope, and I read all of the evidence you gathered against Diamond. Instead of turning it in, I offered her a deal."

I was boiling at this point. "You did what? What type of deal?" I screamed at him.

Diamond interrupted and said, "Nigga, you talking too slow. This is not an episode of *General Hospital*. Let me get to the point. He wanted some pussy. Not only my pussy, though, he wanted a threesome right here. He wanted it today in this room so that Charisma could walk in and see him in the act. It was supposed to be the ultimate payback for her cheating on him with her ex and my get-out-of-jail-free card for you rolling over on me, bitch." She hit me with the butt of the gun across the face.

I immediately felt blood in my mouth. I grabbed my jaw but couldn't do shit at that point. She had the gun. She had the upper hand. I looked at Darnelle and said in pain, "Wait. That doesn't make any sense. I told you to submit the documents. She should have been arrested by now. You fucked up, Darnelle! Now look at us! You a pussy-ass nigga!" I pulled my head back and spit bloody spit into his face. Diamond started laughing.

He took out his neatly folded purple handkerchief, which complemented his all-white tuxedo. "I was still going to submit the file. Oh, this bitch was going to jail for what she did to you, but then you told me that she saved your life. At that point, we knew that she didn't set you up.

Sly planned that on his own accord. I thought for sure you wouldn't want her to go to jail then."

I interrupted and asked, "Then why didn't you tell me that you didn't submit the evidence to have her arrested, Darnelle?"

Laughing, Diamond said, "I'll tell you why. He wanted to keep that leverage on me for a few more hours—just for a few more hours to have his threesome and revenge against your sister. He thought I wouldn't fuck him if he didn't have the evidence over my head. Funny thing is, as fine as he is, I would have fucked him in a minute." She gave him a sexy look.

He stupidly grinned back, blushing as if this bitch weren't going to shoot his dumb ass. They both saw me roll my eyes at them. Then she seductively circled my breasts with the tip of the gun and said, "I would have fucked you too. You always knew I was attracted to you. I've never been with a woman, but you were my exception." I was starting to get sick to my stomach at the thought of her wanting me. I was starting to get a headache, and I knew that when the shock wore off, my jaw was going to start thumping. She continued, "You were supposed to be my partner, Adrianna. I trusted you because you nursed me back to health. I saved you from getting raped and killed, so you knew at that point I didn't try to set you up. You could have told me last night and called Darnelle on our way home to correct the situation. I would have understood. If I was kidnapped by your bother, with our past, I would have thought you were part of the setup as well, at first. However, you found out that I wasn't, and you were still willing to let me go down. You wanted to be the queen of the castle. That's the problem with you, bitch. You hated the fact that Charisma was Darnelle's queen, so you just had to fuck him. I fucked Boss because of him, not because I wanted to get at you. As nice looking as you are, you could have any man. You wanted him even more because he belonged to Charisma. If you would fuck your sister's man, you surely could never be trusted. Once a hoe, always a hoe.

Now you are just like the rest of the hoes in the street. Truth be told, I knew Darnelle's plan was to fuck both of us, have Charisma walk in and see it, and then leave with you. No, he wasn't lying when he told you last night that he chose you, but it was only because Charisma's heart is with someone else.

"So you see, bitch, you are still second choice. You might have had his bed every night, but Charisma still would have had his heart. If he didn't still love her, he wouldn't want to hurt her so bad by having her find him fucking her own sister! He wanted her to hurt like he was hurting. He was a cheater, but he left you alone weeks ago. That meant he was done playing the field. Your dumb ass gets one phone call back after weeks of being ignored, and all of a sudden, you feel special. Bitch, please. You were about to be his get-over-his-last-girl bitch. He was going to use you just to get back at your own sister. You are full of shit, and I'm tired of smelling your ass. Both of you, get on your knees!"

Darnelle and I both got on our knees, bowed our heads, and closed our eyes. Diamond fired twice. Darnelle took two to the chest. I was next. I'd fucked her, and I knew it. She'd fucked me first, but we weren't friends then. She didn't owe me anything. Since we had become friends, she hadn't done anything to screw me. I just hadn't been able to let the fact that she and Boss were sleeping together go, even though I'd wanted to. I had taken the opportunity to pay her back, and it had backfired. She was out for blood, and I couldn't blame her. My life flashed before me. I'd betrayed my sister, and I'd betrayed my best friend, all over a nigga who I'd thought would love me. My mama had always said, "Every smile isn't real, and every 'I love you' isn't true." That day, I learned what that meant.

PART 2

CHAPTER 1

Adrianna

"Run, bitch, before I change my mind," Diamond said as she stood there with tears in her eyes, holding a smoking gun. She was too much of a boss to let a tear drop. She had perfect makeup and flowing, romantic curled hair hanging flawlessly over her shoulders and down her back. She was gorgeous no matter what face she made. She refused to let me or anyone else see her cry. Flashbacks of me washing her hair, while she was recovering from the fall into my fiancé's grave, ran through my mind. I could see in her eyes that she was reflecting on all of the fun we'd had double-dating, going to Beyoncé concerts, and just sitting around having movie nights and cooking each other's favorite dishes for dinner. I knew she was thinking about the times I'd washed her hair when she couldn't wash her own and helped bathe her and put lotion on her until she was able to do it herself. Most importantly, she remembered the thrill we both got from being boss bitches in the drug game, which was usually meant for only niggas to run. When we met with other bosses, when they found out that our set was run by two fine-ass bitches, the looks on their faces were priceless every time. My house had become her house.

Her all-white Chanel pantsuit had bloodstains all over it. She didn't blink or even look at Darnelle's body when it thumped onto the hardwood floor as it fell over. Blood was forming red stains on the chest of his black-and-white tuxedo. His mouth was full of blood, and I had to admit that both of us were full of shit. She was giving me a break, but I knew that this was far from over. I got up off of my knees but didn't move from that spot. I knew that at any moment, she would shoot me if I made the wrong move. I looked down at my left leg and realized it was shaking. I was so busy trying to control my bladder that I didn't notice my hands palms were sweating. Any moment now, someone from the wedding party was going to enter the room and demand to know what had happened.

I didn't want to explain to my sister Charisma that I'd been fucking her fiancé. I didn't want to have to explain that when I was giving him head on their wedding day, the bitch who'd killed him had done so partially because he'd tried to blackmail her to fuck him. I didn't want to see Charisma's face when she found out he'd told Diamond that if she didn't have a ménage à trois with he and I, he would turn over the drug and murder evidence on her—the evidence I'd provided him with when I thought Diamond was in with her brother Sly's attempt to kidnap me and rape me. Only when Diamond shot her brother in the head while he was on top of me had I realized that she had nothing to do with his foolishness. She'd saved my life, and I'd wanted to take hers as payback for sleeping with a nigga who was supposed to be mine but clearly only cared about himself. I had Bossman's heart, but clearly, Diamond had his mind. We had gone from being enemies to being friends and now back to being enemies all in one year.

"Wait!" I said to Diamond, hoping she wouldn't change her mind and just shoot me. "Give me the gun," I whispered, holding my hand out.

"Bitch, is you stuck on stupid? Why would I give you the gun—so you can shoot me?" Diamond said with a serious look on her face.

I reassured her by saying, "No, no. We can say it was self-defense. They will believe me. I can tell my sister that he tried to rape me, and I shot him. So give me the gun, so I can fire it. That way, I can have my fingerprints on it with gun residue on my hands." She still wasn't budging, but she heard people running up the steps from the wedding party, so she understood time was limited. "Diamond, you saved my life. I fucked up. I don't want you to go to jail over this nigga. Charisma is a lawyer. After I tell her what he tried to do, she will never let me see a day in jail." I could see her thinking about it. She loosened her grip on the diamond-studded nine, and I quickly grabbed it and fired twice. I fired up into the ceiling and then dropped the gun just before Charisma, my father, and Rashad came flying into the room.

CHAPTER 2

Nina

Welcome to the missing-persons division. I could have unloaded my entire clip on Chief Raymond for moving me from the homicide division to missing persons after the Banks case. I was persistent in proving that the youngest Banks sister couldn't have killed the victim, due to the trajectory of the bullets. A rookie could have proven that. She had gunpowder on her hands, but four shots were fired. She might have fired the gun, but she didn't fire it at the victim. Darnelle Mitchell was a predominant lawyer. He had looks, power, and money. His family was well known and highly respected because his father was a district-court judge. The evidence didn't add up. I was pulled off the case when I refused to adhere to the order to close the investigation the day after the murder. It was a murder, but the police department told the media it was self-defense. The politics of it all drove me back to drinking.

"Pour me another stiff one, Ahmad," I said, slamming my fifth shot glass down on the bar counter. Ahmad and his older brother ran Blue. Ahmad was handsome like his brother and a smart kid. He had just graduated from high school with a full scholarship to Duke University. His brother had raised him after the death of his parents. I'd heard he had another brother who had been recently killed by the game. "Ahmad, why does your brother always disappear when I come into the bar? Tell him I won't bite unless he wants me to," I said with a wink. His brother was hella fine, and if he was hiding something, I wanted it to remain hidden. I didn't look for crime. I only responded to it when it called.

"I don't know, Detective Ross." He always said the word *detective* with extra emphasis to remind me that he hadn't forgotten who I was, no matter how cool I seemed to be. "Maybe he's scared of your beauty," he said, wiping down the already-spotless counter with a white towel. Then he leaned over the counter in front of me, showing his waves and fresh cut. He always wore a freshly pressed white T-shirt with fresh jeans, nice sneakers, diamonds in his ears, and a nice diamond watch in the daytime. At night, he would switch to a neatly pressed collared black dress shirt and black slacks with the same accessories.

"I don't blame him. If I wasn't a cop, I wouldn't fuck with them either," I said, laughing. He thought it was hilarious as well and was smiling, showing his perfect white teeth. "You have that clean, pretty-boy swag, I see, Ahmad. You got a girlfriend?" I asked.

"Nah, I'm too focused on my books, working, and working out. I only have a partial basketball scholarship and a one-year academic scholarship to Duke," he said, grabbing a bottled water to drink. It was getting busy, but thanks to the other bartenders, Malcolm and Akia, we were able to talk for a little bit longer. "They come at me, but after losing my parents, I just don't want to be connected to anyone. It's easier to go on with your future when you're not connected to anyone from your past, Detective," he said with a half-smile.

"Don't let college turn you out," I said, joking.

Laughing, he said, "In college, I will obtain my education to better my future and find my wife to spend it with. Too many men let hoes bring them down, chasing after the pussy. I trust no one, so the one I do decide to trust is going to be my wife. When was the last time you heard a wife selling out a husband who has been good to her? But a hoe—a hoe will roll on you eventually, no matter how good the nigga is. I've seen it happen too many times. It ain't worth it to me," he said with a serious look on his face.

"Damn, Ahmad, I didn't know you were going to go that deep. You almost blew my buzz!" We both started cracking up.

"Here's one on the house. Stay sexy, Detective," he said, and he disappeared into the back. I assumed he was going to change into his signature all-black nightlife outfit. Blue was jumping, as it always was on Friday nights. It had a Philly swag that drew in a lot of Northerners turned Southerners all day every day. In Philly, bars were open and packed all day long. Most of the bars in Charlotte didn't open up until four in the afternoon and didn't get crowded until after seven. However, Blue was the top spot to hit for the African American community. Whether one was old or young, Blue was starting to be the place where everyone went to get away. It had a little bit of everything on the low. At the entrance, to the left was the bar, where they sold the best fish and chicken. There were a couple of booths and round tables to the right, and on the other side was a room with four pool tables. Directly down the middle was a deep red curtain that concealed the dance floor behind it. That was where the crowd headed when they heard their song come on. During the day, the bar played all of the best old-school music, from Otis Redding to Luther Vandross. Between six and seven, karaoke began. After eight, the new-school music started, and after ten on Friday and Saturday nights, the only thing playing was booty-shaking music. That was when the top-of-the-line Atlanta and Charlotte strippers took advantage of the poles. Most of them were college girls from the surrounding cities. A&T, JCSU, Clark Atlanta, and Spellman were just a few of the historically black colleges that surrounded the Queen City of Charlotte. I'd graduated from Clark Atlanta and then moved to Charlotte. I'd been there ever since.

After my free drink, I grabbed my items and called Seth to tell him to meet me back at my apartment for an all-nighter.

CHAPTER 3

Jullian

A hoe was going to be a hoe no matter what. That was why I kept hoes out of my circle. However, you had no choice about keeping a hoe around when that hoe was family. That was called a family hoe. Every family had one. If you thought your family didn't, then you were probably the hoe. You just had to remember the golden rule: never let a hoe be around your man alone under any circumstances. If he was in the kitchen during Thanksgiving dinner and the family hoe was there, then you were in the kitchen. If your man was still up, chatting it up with the boys, on Christmas Eve, then you were still up on Christmas Eve. If he woke up to use the family bathroom, then you woke up and acted as if you had to use the bathroom. If you gave the family hoe no breathing room, he wouldn't smell her scent. You shouldn't even tell him that she was the family hoe, because curiosity would kill the cat. Then you would have to kill him. Doing these things would not necessarily stop your man from cheating, but it would stop that man from cheating with that hoe. If a man decided to cheat, you, as the woman, got more credibility if he cheated with an outside hoe. You got zero respect if he cheated with the family hoe, because you knew she was a hoe from the beginning, and you let your man be around her unattended.

PREVIEW OF
C.R.E.A.M.

············ ⧢ ············

CHAPTER 1

The Beginning

The only thing worse than a man in these streets was a woman in these streets. I'd tried to do the right thing all my life. I received a half academic and half basketball scholarship to University of Florida and ranked in the top five percent for basketball. I earned my degree in accounting, but because of some unfortunate situations, I was now using my degree to count drug money and bodies. Those who made it got paid, and those who didn't got laid. We didn't take prisoners, nor did we let them return home. That was just the way the game was set up. You were either in, or you were out, but once you said you were in, you were in until death. Family came first unless they were proven to be disloyal. Loyalty was everything. So snitches didn't get stitches; they got bagged.

"Please! Don't hurt me! I'm so sorry!" she pleaded with snot rolling down her face and tears falling, making her mascara run. I was sure her head was pounding as I dragged her across the rooftop by her hair. The cement was scraping her long legs, leaving a trail of blood all the way to the ledge. "I will do anything as long as you let me live. I never meant for it to go this far. I promise you I didn't. Please!"

Her pleas could not drown my anger or the hurt in my heart. She had taken everything from me that I valued most, so I was going to take what she valued most—herself. I was at the point of no return. No man could have stopped me, not even me. When we got to the brick ledge, I looked into her face, showing no remorse, because I had none at the time. She was full of fear but understood there was nothing more she could say. Her eyes were full of tears as I lifted her up with my hand still wrapped around her hair. She wore only a black Victoria's Secret bra and panties, which the street below would see in a few minutes. She still looked perfect on the outside, but she was evil on the inside. It did not matter at this point if she was sincere in her apology. She had to pay the ultimate price. "Eye for an eye, remember?" were the last words I said before I threw her over the ledge and into the uptown Charlotte night traffic. She screamed for the first few seconds. When she fell silent right before I expected her body to land, I turned around and walked away. It had to be done. *Fuck her.*

"How dare they show us an apartment without an elevator in it? My last name alone should have told them that was unacceptable," Miracle said as she rolled her eyes and turned her nose up at the Realtor. She was so busy stomping her red-soled shoes across the hardwood flooring that she didn't notice the way I was staring into the eyes of my future wife.

I had known she was the one the moment she'd peeked her head around the door as she opened it to welcome us, saying, "Welcome, Mr. Strong and Ms. Rich." Her eyes were humble, deep, mysterious, and sexy. There was a light that surrounded her, and she was glowing. When I smiled, she smiled. I hadn't even looked at her body yet. I was too captured by her beauty. In that moment, I knew she was the one. When we walked in, she immediately started walking to the great room to show us the view of the city. The Atmore penthouse apartment had a spectacular view of uptown Charlotte and the Panthers stadium. I loved it immediately, although my eyes were really focused on the behind and hips of the woman in front of me. Her pinstriped pencil skirt looked professionally painted on. When she turned around, my heart stopped, and I practically went into shock for a moment. Doing a half turn in her stilettos like a ballerina, she asked, "So how do you like the view?"

She was pregnant. I estimated her to be about five months along. I couldn't help but think, *She was too good to be true.*

"I love the view. I can see all of Charlotte from here. My father would be proud, baby. What do you think?" Miracle asked as she tried to grab my hand. I pretended I didn't see her trying to grab it and acted as if I had interest in seeing the view much closer. I stood beside the Realtor, admiring her view from head to toe. I heard Miracle walk into the kitchen. She was talking, but I heard nothing she said until she walked back in about two minutes later, complaining about not having an elevator. In those two minutes that she was gone, the Realtor and I connected emotionally. I smiled, and then she smiled. She smiled, and then I smiled. Then we just looked at each other, imagining how it would be to be with one another.

"What is your first name, Ms. Jordan?" I asked, admiring her full lips and long, bone-straight black hair.

"Jada," she said, smiling, showing her beautiful teeth and a dimple on her right check. She gave me her business card—in case we wanted to see more houses, she said. But Miracle already had her business card. I knew then that giving me the card was her way of saying, "Call me."

"After viewing the rest of the penthouse, I would love to take you up to the rooftop. It is available by appointment only. It has a pool, a Jacuzzi, a dining table for four, and the most beautiful view, especially at night, from all sides of the Atmore Building."

Printed in the United States
By Bookmasters